HIDDEN IN THE HILLS

CATHIE LAMPKIN

ISBN: 1535003502
ISBN-13:9781535003506
Library of Congress Control Number: 2016911163
CreateSpace Independent Publishing Platform, North Charleston, SC

Bilocation- the state of being or ability to be in two places at the same time.

PROLOGUE

Angelina Bernardo Pasquali's brother Carmine was having multiple affairs and no amount of pleading from her would stop him. All she could do was hope that his seed would not take hold.

She and Carmine never got along. Not only was he a bully and a cad, he defied their parents and society at every turn. The black sheep of the family, as it were. Carmine refused the arranged marriage. And because he was ever aware of his own mortality, he did his best to pollute the family line and the objects of his "affections" were married women. Angelina supposed he thought it an easy place to hide the family "gold".

Soon after Carmine's early, yet not surprising death, she knew. And although she had the great gift of precognition, it was not her strongest trait. Angelina did not know which child he would sire. She did, however, "know" that only one child would come to term.

Tina, once Angelina's friend, showed pregnant first, and bore a son. Tina would deny an affair, of course, not risking social disgrace. It surprised Angelina that no one ever questioned why Anthony, Tina eldest son, had striking good looks which his younger brother would never possess, or why the eldest had suffered rashes and headaches and an early death.

Characteristics, of course, in the Bernardo family males.

No one was ever suspicious.

No one, except Angelina.

She had started to write numerous letters to Tina over the years, all of them written on elegant, expensive, imported Italian stationary. She was never able to bring herself to send them. After all, she wouldn't be able prove it. Tina would never admit to the affair and Angelina had her own son, Michael, to protect. So, never absolutely sure, she wrote one final note and left it in the safe. This note was not for Tina but for the grandson she would never get to know.

CHAPTER 1 ✿

"Just another day in paradise," Christine Smith said out loud to no one.

She was pleased that her dollar store sunglasses managed to cut out most of the brilliant morning sun. She gently punched in the knob on the radio and music from The Eagle's filled her used Geo Tracker.

"…there were voices down the corridor; I thought I heard them say…"

Around the bend was a small orange grove and she strained as she cranked down the squeaky window allowing the blossom's fragrance to engulf her car.

Singing along with the song, she breathed in the heavily perfumed air.

"…Some dance to remember, some dance to forget…."

Christine often found herself absorbed in songs. This one in particular was a favorite. She imagined herself walking in a moonlit garden on a warm summer evening.

"…We're all just prisoners here, of our own device," she sang.

"That was 'Hotel California'- from thirty years ago in 1976, here on oldies 104.5," the DJ announced. "It's a quarter of nine on a picture perfect February day. Highs today will be in the lower to mid 70s with low humidity and zero percent chance of rain here in Sarasota. If you can, get out and enjoy this beautiful weather. *This* is why we live here…."

"Isn't *that* the truth!" Christine answered back to the radio. She pulled the Tracker into her numbered parking space, got out, and headed towards the administration building of the private middle school. She brought with her a bag lunch and white cardigan sweater. She had only been in Florida for a few months, and welcomed the warm weather, but prepared for the blast of cold air at exactly eleven o'clock each and every morning when the thermostat on the air conditioner dropped.

On her way to a small, unpretentious office at the far end of the hallway, she stopped to get her mail in the mailroom.

"Good morning Tonya. What a beautiful day!"

"Why, it sure is!" replied the pint sized, red-haired receptionist. "How are you doing this morning, Christine?"

"Very well, thank you. How are you?"

"Terrific! It's payday!" Tonya replied excitedly, waving a green check at her.

Of the few pieces of paper that she removed from her mailbox, Christine noticed a neat white envelope with her name scribbled on it. She opened it immediately.

"I guess I'll have to get used to the cost of living difference down here," she sighed with disappointment as she reviewed her first paycheck. Even though it covered several weeks of work, it was still miserably small. But she was hoping to move into a small efficiency apartment soon, and this would be more than enough for the security deposit. She was quickly getting tired of the tiny room she was renting for the last few months. Transferring funds from her savings account to her checking account was going to be commonplace for a while.

Tonya consoled her, "That teaching position will come up soon, honey, don't worry."

"Christine, come to my office!" a voice boomed from behind them.

Christine turned around to see Martha Moore, the administrative assistant to the principal, who had rudely interrupted them.

Mad Martha, as some of the secretaries called her when she was out of earshot, looked rather like a cross between a thin alien and a praying mantis. Her upper body leaned forward as she walked and her nose pointed up in the air like a drug-sniffing dog. She always wore black, and her clothing draped loosely on her tall and bony frame.

Tonya spat out a simple greeting.

"Martha." She was clearly irritated by the unprofessional interruption. Christine sensed friction between them.

"Tonya." Martha replied curtly.

"Hey, Martha," Christine stammered, "I, well, I have a few things I need to get in order in my office, then I can come by."

"As soon as you can," Martha sidled back through the doorway as silently as she'd entered.

"What do you suppose she wants?" Christine asked Tonya.

Two female teachers entered the room, after finishing up a conversation they'd had in the hall and began sorting through the papers in their mailboxes.

"Who knows with Martha," Tonya warned. "Maybe you have more papers to sign. Just be careful around her. She could make things 'real ugly' for you with Mr. Holsten. You want that teaching job don't you?"

"What do you mean?" Christine was assured by the Principal, Mr. Holsten, during her interview that she would be able to fill the next teaching position available but would have to work as the assistant to the counselor until the next spot opened.

"She tends to abuse her position here. I've seen her do it lots of times. She'll stick her nose in your business. Then she'll decide if she likes you or not. Then if she doesn't, look out," Tonya said.

"But how can that be? The Principal hired me. Martha's just a secretary. If I do my job, she can't hurt me, right?"

"At most other schools that would be true, but not here."

"What do you mean?"

"If she doesn't like you, she'll squeeze you out."

"How?"

"She'll make it so you can't do your work. I've seen her asking around for help with her projects. But you won't be 'helping out' at all. You'll have to take over the entire project with all the responsibilities and time invested and none of the pay and certainly no support from her. Martha's making some big bucks while doing very little. And she'll happily take credit for your original ideas but quick to blame you if there's a problem," Tonya said bitterly. "Right, Alice?" Tonya asked the pretty teacher with long brown hair and green eyes.

"I've seen her meddlin' and tellin' others how to do their jobs, while complainin' she can't get any of her own work done," Alice said with a thick southern accent. "She'll play the martyr in front of Mr. Holsten, stayin' late and makin' all that overtime."

"How can she have so much influence?" Christine asked.

"Apparently, Martha has an 'in' with Mr. Holsten," the other teacher offered, organizing her papers into two neat stacks.

"Or maybe he's afraid of her, too," Alice said in a hushed voice, glancing over at her friend who acknowledge her with a nod. "We teachers try to have as little contact with her as possible."

"Very disagreeable," the other teacher added before both teachers left the room.

"Sometimes, bullies never grow up," Tonya stated, quickly glancing up at the clock on the wall. "Be careful, Christine."

CHAPTER 2 ❁

While his eleven-year-old daughter Shelly, fidgeted beside him, Joseph Pasquali sat quietly on the plane bound for Orlando. He reanalyzed a map of Italy, trying to become familiar with the country and the little villages he highlighted in neon green.

"Take some time," his doctors had encouraged him. "Get away for a while. Take a trip. Reduce the stress in your life."

"Will a trip help with my prognosis?" Joe had asked sarcastically, already knowing it would not.

Joe had planned this trip several weeks ago, and it was not for pleasure. Not for him, anyway. He was running out of time. Finding resolution in Italy to ensure his daughter's future was his goal.

As a single father, Joe was having difficulty raising a daughter. Shelly's mother had gotten pregnant on purpose in order to marry him. Joe had realized too late that all she'd wanted was his money. He also knew that there was no way that this woman would be able to handle the secret. His attorney quietly took care of the divorce and the woman, and Joe received full custody of Shelly.

Shelly was now as precocious as any other preteen. He couldn't tell if it was the emerging hormones or the exposure to the Institute's testing that created Shelly's occasional hysterics and wild mood swings. He was thankful for the help of the female employees at MIRC, especially Teresa. They all cared for Shelly and were always happy to help him out.

He felt comfortable leaving Shelly with Rita, a former associate now living in Orlando, for the few days he would be in Italy. He hoped a break from the pressures of the place and the nastiest winter New Jersey had ever experienced would be good for both of them.

Joe felt the plane tilt and bounce slightly and sensed the other passengers' uneasiness as several hands rose to request an alcoholic beverage. Shelly also started to get irritable and jumpy in her seat.

"Shelly, please sit still. Why don't you look at all of those brochures you brought or how about the book you have on Disney and read? We're almost there."

"I can't get comfortable!" Shelly complained, squirming in her seat. "I wish we were in first class. The seats are bigger and there's more room. *We* should have gone first class!"

"Shelly, you know why we couldn't. Anyway, it's been a short three-hour flight. Look, we're just about there. Try to relax and think about what a great time you're going to have with Rita at Disney World."

Still wiggling, Shelly rolled her big blue eyes at her father.

Another bump followed by a "ding" sound as the *Fasten Seatbelt* sign lit up. The pilot's voice crackled through the overhead speakers.

"This is Captain Anderson," he said casually. "Well, folks, looks like we've got a few stray showers ahead of us and so I've turned on the 'fasten seatbelt sign'. For your safety please remain in your seats for the remainder of the flight." The PA sputtered for a moment as the pilot paused, then added, "We will be starting our final descent into Orlando in just a few minutes. The weather in Orlando this morning is a warm 72 degrees under partly cloudy skies." The PA crackled out.

"I have to go to the bathroom."

"Now?" Joe sighed as he flipped over his left wrist and glanced at the Rolex under his sleeve. "We'll be on the ground in a few minutes. Can't you wait? You can use the restrooms in the airport. Besides, looks like it's gonna be bumpy and the pilot just said we are to stay in our seats."

"I don't feel right, something's wrong, I need to go. I need to get up and go to the bathroom or something..." Shelly stammered, unclipped her seat belt and quickly stepped out into the aisle.

CHAPTER 3 ✿

"Sit down for a minute, will you?" Martha said, closing the door behind Christine. Straight black hair with frizzy gray strands spiraling out hung long around thick plastic framed eyes.

Martha's office was in sharp contrast to her personality. Her office was full of beauty and light. It was a large office with a big and bright window. The room was completely filled with different varieties of orchids, several already having an open bloom. They were everywhere, hanging from above, sitting on the ledge, and even covering much of Martha's desk.

Taking a seat, Christine commented on the beautiful flowers, attempting to build rapport.

"Your plants are lovely."

"They're orchids," Martha immediately corrected her. "These require special care and attention to make them look this wonderful." A terracotta pot with a twelve inch tall plant in it sat closest to her, next to her computer. She touched its single pink flower gently. "My precious babies. This one is my favorite and it just opened," she pouted as she puffed a kiss at it, nearly nauseating Christine.

"Did anyone tell you that I have a special 'hut' in my backyard so I can grow some of the most exotic orchids available," Martha bragged. "Sometimes I even hire a private guard for certain times of the year when some of my most rare and expensive flowers bloom!"

Not exactly sure how to respond to the clearly obsessed woman, Christine merely replied, "You are very dedicated."

Martha's tone suddenly changed and right away Christine felt Martha's dislike for her.

"I need for you to help me out with a project, Christine."

… *help me out*….Christine sucked in her breath, recalling the warning she had just received in the mailroom.

"We have Bereavement Group here at this school. I had volunteered to be Staff Coordinator this year, but I now find that I simply don't have the time. You will be taking over the club," Martha said, matter-of-factly. "Here's the paperwork," she said, and pushed a manila envelope across her desk around the pot holding the pink orchid.

Christine noticed that the seal hadn't even been broken.

"It's a rather large group, unfortunately, parents as well as children," Martha continued coldly. "Just read it. I'm sure you can figure it all out."

"Bereavement Club? You mean children who've lost a parent?"

"Yes. They've lost a parent, sibling, pet, whatever," Martha replied coldly.

Christine was taken aback by Martha's total lack of empathy and she stammered, "Martha, listen, I'm flattered, really, but I'm certainly not qualified for this. I'm afraid I can't help you."

"You don't have to be qualified; you just have to be an employee. I'm so busy and I have a lot of responsibilities around here. Someone has to take this over. They assigned it to me but..."

Christine pushed back in her chair and cocked her head catching Martha in the lie. She hadn't "volunteered" at all. She was *assigned* the job and was now passing it off onto her.

Martha, noting that she had been caught, tried to cover, "Anyway, of course you can do it. I've seen you with the children. They seem to like you," she said bitterly.

"No, Martha, you don't understand," Christine said anxiously. "A large group all struggling with a loss….I really, *really* can't take this on…"

Christine had carefully selected Corwin Academy for its small class sizes. She had issues dealing with large groups and certainly knew she was unable to deal with groups in pain.

"*Yes,* you can." Martha persisted, her voice tightened, her black, deep-set eyes darkened. "I understand that you are interested in a teaching position…?" Martha's voice trailed off.

Even though Christine had great empathy and compassion for children in middle school, she knew that there was no way she could be involved with this club. No way. And while doing her best not to irritate Martha any more, she tried to explain. "I really would like to help you out, Martha, really I would but, you see, I 'm not…"

"Good. Then it's settled." Martha said cutting her off and pushing the envelope further across the desk.

Christine pleaded, "Listen, Martha, I'm not good…, I.," she stammered, "I… I can't be with groups under this kind of stress. I'd really like to help but I just can't do this! I can't be responsible for…." Christine stopped mid-sentence, remembering an incident a few years back when she attended a Veteran's Day celebration.

She had attended a ceremony in a small church and it was the first time she'd felt those "strange feelings." The air got heavy, and she could feel the intense pain that was all around her. Feelings of extreme sadness and also confinement overwhelmed her. Heaviness engulfed her and she couldn't breathe. She'd become lightheaded and eventually passed out. She was more embarrassed than anything else, and ever since then she avoided places where people harboring strong emotions gathered.

Squirming in her chair Christine continued, "I have a full plate, Martha. Surely, you can understand. I'm sorry, but I can't really help you with this club."

Christine rose from her chair and slowly started to back out of the room. Martha's face hardened like stone.

"This is not up for debate, Christine. You *will* do this." Martha said, glaring at her, eyes smoldering black coals inside concrete gray skin.

Christine felt a cold shiver run up her spine, her heart raced and her face burned with anger. How she hated confrontation!

The room suddenly got cold. They both shivered. Christine looked at the digital clock on Martha's desk. The red L.E.D. numbers indicted that it was only 9:29, too early for the air-conditioning to start.

Christine sorely resented being bullied. She turned on her heals and fled the room, hating herself for not being more assertive. Behind her, Martha's grin was quickly replaced by dismay as the orchid on her desk released it precious solitary pink bloom onto the untouched manila envelope.

CHAPTER 4✿

Christine was reeling and couldn't remember the last time she'd been this agitated. She was trying to breathe and regain her self-control.

Heading back to her office, Christine slowed her pace as she noticed a young girl near the end of the hall with wavy blond hair and large blue eyes standing stiffly, as if frozen. The girl was staring straight down the hall at her, mouth gaping open, arms at her sides, not speaking, or moving.

Christine had been working at the small middle school for about two months and had seen most of the students, but she did not recognize this pretty little girl. Christine called out to her, "Honey, are you all right?"

The girl did not respond. Christine took two more steps towards her and abruptly stopped. All of a sudden she felt as if she were in the ocean being pulled by a strong current; the water pushing heavy against her body. She couldn't move. Her feet were planted as if deep in sand and the hairs on her arms and the back of her neck stood upright. A thick fog suddenly appeared in the school hallway.

What is this?

The thunderous whirl of engines startled her. She could hear muffled sounds of coughs and smelled stale re-circulated air. *What's happening?* Her mind screamed. One minute she was speaking to the child and the next she was --on a plane! The girl was still in front of her, but they weren't in the school anymore, *they were both on a plane!* Everything around her was blurred and distorted. Everything except the girl. The girl was as clear and sharp as could be.

Christine found herself standing in the aisle holding onto the seats in front of her. She could feel the coarse material under her fingertips. Mechanically she reached up and touched the hard, cold, unforgiving plastic of the luggage holders above the seats. She had tunnel vision. The edges of everything were fuzzy. She could hear a woman's voice over the engine's drone, speaking to her seat mate. Christine couldn't make out many of the words, but every time the women said a word with the letter "s" in it, Christine could hear the "sssss".

"...sso then sshe ssaid,...ssee, it's like thisss........sshe wass sso sstupid, sso then sshe...ssaid..."

A baby was crying... somewhere in front of her to the right. She couldn't see the baby, but the wail escalated. Christine was frustrated by the fog and blur of the tunnel vision. The only thing she saw clearly was the girl in front of her, wide eyed and staring *at* and *behind* Christine.

Christine turned around to see what the girl was looking at and saw a man in his early to middle thirties in a dark suit standing in the aisle a few feet behind her. He was facing toward the front of the plane and she was able to see his features quite clearly. She noticed that he had an old fashioned handlebar mustache. Then he reached into his jacket and she saw a silver glint. He pulled out a small handgun. Suddenly, he got a crazed look on his face as if suddenly surprised. For a split second, Christine thought he was going to shoot her, but it was as if he didn't even *see* her. He was looking *through* her. Then, to her horror, Christine realized that he was going to shoot this young girl!

"NO!" Christine screamed and lunged towards the man.

They fell as she grabbed his arm and struggled for the gun. She could hear the passengers screaming. The baby's shrieking was ear splitting. The whirl of the engines changing speed was deafening. The plane dipped and pitched.

Panic and fear overwhelmed her. She felt the heavy pressure of the confined space squeezing against her chest and lungs. Just before she blacked out she heard the gun go off.

Robin, the school counselor Christine worked for, came out of her office and into the hallway. She noticed Christine walking slowly and deliberately, wavering ever so slightly, then Christine turned towards her and screamed "NO!"

Robin stopped immediately and watched in shock as Christine took a few steps and then suddenly lunged at her, forcing the counselor to stumble backwards into her office. She saw Christine open her arms wide then close them around herself, falling to the floor, thrashing about.

"Someone help!" Robin cried.

Christine rocked on the floor for a moment then went limp.

Tonya appeared immediately.

"I don't know what happened to her! She just collapsed!" Robin said to Tonya. "Get the nurse, quick!"

Within seconds the nurse arrived and a small crowd had started to gather in the hallway. Christine had completely stopped moving and was lying on her side. The school nurse carefully turned her onto her back and checked for breathing.

"She probably just tripped over her own feet," Martha spat, hovering in the back of the crowd.

"Christine! Christine, can you hear me?" shouted the nurse. She gently shook Christine's shoulders, and suddenly saw the blood soaking thru Christine's yellow polo shirt.

"She's bleeding!" the nurse exclaimed. Continuing to try to revive Christine she demanded, "Did anyone see what happened?"

CHAPTER 5✿

"...And the rest of you are free to go," the officer finally announced after asking a select few to remain on board for further questioning. "There are airport escorts waiting in the terminal to assist those of you who require further travel arrangements. Sorry about the delay," he said. "Unfortunately, these investigations take time."

"Dad, we're in Tampa! How are we supposed to get to Orlando?" Shelly argued at the airline desk when they were told there were no more flights going to Orlando that day.

"Listen, sweetheart, this airport was more equipped to handle this emergency. Orlando isn't that far away. I'll get you there tomorrow, I promise. I think we've had enough excitement for one day."

Joe noticed a large crowd of people and TV cameras bustling down the corridor.

"Speaking of excitement..." Joe said and took Shelly in one hand and his luggage in the other.

"Grab your stuff, we're outa here!"

Shelly grabbed the handle of her new rolling suitcase and off they went, desperately trying to avoid the media.

Finally outside in the Florida sunshine, Joe quickly hailed a cab and checked into a nearby airport hotel.

He then phoned Rita and briefly explained what had happened.

"I'm sure she's frightened. No sense putting the child back on a plane," Rita said. "Why don't you see if you can reschedule your flight to Italy from Tampa? I'm anxious to see you and Shelly. What if I come out and meet you for breakfast in the morning? We'll catch up and I'll drive Shelly back myself," Rita offered.

Joe thought for a moment and agreed that it was a good idea. He thanked Rita and after they hung up, he managed to reschedule his flight.

After the arrangements were made he turned to Shelly and asked, "How about some dinner? I'm starving. How about you? You must be hungry."

She had been looking out the window, watching the sunset fade and listening to his conversation with Rita. "Can we order room service?" Shelly asked without turning around.

"Sure, where's the menu?"

Once their order was placed, Shelly asked, "Dad? I still don't understand some of what happened."

"What don't you understand, darlin'?" Joe walked over to the window and looked at the beautiful evening sky. Palm trees appeared in dark shadows against the skyline.

"How'd he do it? How'd he get on the plane with a gun?"

"I don't know. I don't understand that either. I only thank goodness that no one was hurt!"

"How come the police didn't talk to us?"

"We were pretty far up front. The police wanted to interview the passengers who were the closest. They have the guy in custody, and the gun, and several good eyewitnesses saying they all saw the same thing. That's all they need."

"What about the lady?"

"What lady?"

"The lady that saved me."

Joe looked hard at his daughter.

"What do you mean, saved you? What are you talking about, Shelly?" He took a deep breath and felt his heart lurch in his chest. With great hesitancy he asked, "Did you *do* something?"

"I just knew you'd say that!" Shelly said insolently. "No Dad, I didn't. Honest, I didn't. But I thought he was going to shoot *me*. Then I saw the lady. She jumped at him and knocked him down."

"I don't understand, Shelly. Here, sit down," Joe gently put his hands on his daughter's shoulders and sat her down on the edge of the bed then pulled over a nearby chair for himself.

"First of all, why would someone want to shoot you? He couldn't have known who we are. Even if he did, why would he want to hurt you?" The thought that his daughter may have been in danger crept into his head and Joe felt the subtle whirl in his brain begin and faint lights began to flash in and out.

"I don't know. He *was* looking at me and then the lady tackled him!"

"Honey, maybe you saw a lady get out of the way or something. When I heard the commotion I pulled you down. I looked back and saw the guy. He was seizing on the floor. Alone. Then two men jumped on him and contained him until we landed."

"What happened to the lady?"

"I don't know what lady you're talking about. I'm sure the police interviewed everyone involved and your 'lady', whoever you saw, is just fine. The guy was heading for the front of the plane, probably to the cockpit, not you," Joe added, trying to console her. "Look, it's been a long day and we're both really tired. Why don't you see if there's a good movie on and I'll go get us some soda? We'll talk more after you rest a bit and eat something."

She shrugged as he hugged her and handed her the remote. The thick, coarse bed spread made a shuffling noise as she scooted back. The pillows were soft and she piled several behind her so that she could lean against the headboard.

"I'll be right back," he called over his shoulder, hearing her start to flip through the channels.

Ice bucket and key in hand, Joe left the room.

Why would she think she was in danger? Joe worried. He took all of the necessary precautions, and then some. Joe tried to convince himself that the pilot was the intended target. But Shelly *was* in the aisle. Joe hadn't seen any 'lady'. Why would she make it up, he wondered.

The cans of soda ricocheting through the machine increased the pressure building in his head.

Shelly flipped through the channels and was disappointed to find that one of her favorite Disney movies, *Confessions of a Teenage Drama Queen*, had just ended. She continued to channel surf.

Within moments Joe was back and met the bellhop at the door.

"Shelly?" he called into the room. "Come get the ice and sodas."

Shelly promptly set down the remote, jumped off the bed and went to help her father at the door.

"Thank you, sir," the waiter replied as he accepted the ten-dollar tip Joe offered.

Joe took the tray of cheeseburgers and fries into the room. Shelly was pouring the two grape sodas at a table in front of the TV when the evening newscast began.

"A Georgia man is in police custody tonight after firing a weapon on Continental flight 1064 from Newark to Orlando. The plane made an emergency landing at Tampa International Airport today..."

Joe and Shelly both sat at the table and watched in silence.

"...Sources say Dr. Kenneth Blyme, age 35 from Harriet's Bluff, Georgia, smuggled a small .22 caliber handgun on board. The gunman fired once before he appeared to suffer a seizure. Several passengers were able to contain Blyme until he was taken into custody by the police. No one on board was injured. The plane remains grounded until the authorities recover the bullet. No further information is available at this time." The picture of a man with a handlebar mustache momentarily flashed on the screen. The young blond anchorwomen made her segue to the weatherman.

"Yup, that's the guy," Shelly said, stuffing her mouth with French Fries. "Why do they have to find the bullet, Dad?"

"Well, the police know that a bullet was actually fired. They're looking for the bullet to make sure there's no damage to the plane. They can't use the plane again until they find it."

"Good thing it didn't go through a window. We all might have been sucked out -like in the movies!" Shelly announced with a giggle.

Yeah, just like in the movies, Joe thought, realizing she had no idea how serious this situation could have been.

After the weather and several commercials, the female anchor came on again as Joe and Shelly were stacking the dinner dishes back on the tray.

"...in other news, Corwin Academy in Sarasota went into lockdown for several hours this morning after an employee apparently sustained a gunshot wound in the Administration Building. No students were present at the time and no one else was injured. The wounded employee is Christine Smith....."

"Daddy, that's her!" Shelly cried, dropping several plastic dishes on the floor when she saw the driver's license photo on the TV. "That's the lady on the plane! The one I tried to tell you about..." she exclaimed. "Daddy, that's the lady I saw on the plane!"

"What? Who...her?" Joe stammered, twisting his head from the TV to Shelly and back to the TV again. "She wasn't on the plane. Didn't you hear? She works at an area school? She was *at* the school this morning when we were on the plane."

"ssshhhhh…wait!" Shelly frantically waved her hand at her father. A thin, well dressed reporter holding a microphone in his hand appeared in front of a brightly lit school building.

"…Rob Tiner is on location in Sarasota tonight at the Middle School with an update. Rob, it looks quiet on campus. Can you give us an update? What's happening at the school?"

"Yes, Carol, all of the students and staff members are accounted for and none of them were involved in this apparent shooting. The school's administrative staff and police are still present on campus. What we know is this…" The reporter continued. "When medics arrived this morning, they found Ms. Smith unconscious and bleeding from a possible gunshot wound. The school immediately went into a lockdown while authorities secured the campus. Once the grounds were thoroughly searched and no suspect was found, parents were called and allowed to pick up their children and buses were called in to transport the remaining students home…"

Joe shook his head and felt comforted that Shelly was privately tutored on the grounds of the institute. She was isolated, but she was safe.

"What do we know about the victim, Rob?" Carol asked as the snapshot of Christine again appeared in the corner of the screen.

"Dad….that *is* her! I *know* it is!" Shelly shouted in hysterics. "She was on the plane. She's the one!"

"…Ms. Smith was transported to Sarasota Memorial where she remains in fair condition this evening. She is expected to make a full recovery. Not very much is known about her. She's only been with the school system for a short time and as far as we know, has no local family members we could find to speak with."

"And a suspect? What are police saying?"

"Police have no suspects at this time. Witnesses told police they didn't see anyone enter or leave the building at the time of the incident, and the school administration told us they immediately went into lockdown. Police are unable to determine how Miss Smith sustained a gunshot injury. Corwin Academy will be closed tomorrow while this investigation continues. Authorities hope to have more information when the ballistics report comes back."

"I don't know why I'm the only one who saw her, but I did and that's her! And she's hurt. He shot her, dad!" Shelly cried and stomped her foot.

"Wait...hold on...just settle down. Let me think a minute." Joe stammered, unnerved and unable to control his daughter's outbursts.

"Someone can't be in two places at the same time, Shelly," He felt the nervous knot in his stomach grow and headed for his medicine, still in his unopened, unpacked suitcase.

"She was there. I saw her! You have to believe me this time. She was there!" Afraid he wouldn't believe her, Shelly persisted, "I'm *not* lying this time and I didn't *do* anything. Everything happened so fast; I wouldn't have had any time, even if I wanted to. Sometimes, even when I *am* telling the truth, you don't believe me."

The institution taught her well, Joe thought. Keeping secrets was a necessity. It pained him to see her struggle to walk the fine line between lying and keeping secrets.

Shelly stomped toward the bathroom and stormed by the tray of dinner dishes that her father had piled up and set on the dresser. They clamored together loudly.

"And I didn't do *that*, either!" She said and slammed the bathroom door.

"I didn't say I didn't believe you." Joe said at the closed door. "I'm sure there's some explanation."

Shelly was more composed after her shower. Joe was proud of her for trying to manage her emotions.

"Look, honey, you've had a long day. Everything's going to be fine," Joe reassured his daughter. "We're safe and no one is going to hurt you. Rita will be here in the morning to drive you to Orlando. Get some rest. You're going to have a great time at Disney," he consoled her as he tucked her into the double bed next to his. "I love you honey, sweet dreams."

"I love you too, Daddy." Shelly threw her arms around her father's neck, hugged him tight and kissed him on the cheek. "I hope that lady is going to be okay," she whispered, closing her eyes and melting into the pillow. Shelly's breathing slowed and soon she was fast asleep.

Joe checked the door, making sure it was double locked. He took a quick shower and after he was confident that Shelly was deeply asleep, he made one more phone call-- the one call he had been thinking about most of the evening.

CHAPTER 6 ❀

Joe dialed the long distance number and waited for the familiar voice to answer the phone.

"MIRC. How may I direct your call?"

"Hi, Cheryl, it's Joe."

"Joe, how ah ya? How's the weatha in Florida?" his secretary asked in her deep Jersey drawl.

"It's nice. Warm… Listen, we had a little trouble on the plane and we're spending the night in Tampa."

"Oh, I'm sorry to hea that. I hope it wasn't Shelly."

"No, it wasn't Shelly."

"Well, I hope your flight to Italy is betta. Enjoy the sun, down thea. We're expecting anotha couple a inches a snow before tomorra. So, how can I help, Joe?"

"May I speak to Teresa, please… if she's still around?"

"Yea, she's still hea, hold on while I track a down."

"Thanks Cheryl."

"Always a pleasha, Joe. Good luck in Italy. I hope ya find what ya looking for," replied Cheryl as she patched him through.

"Hey, Joe, what's goin' on down there?" Teresa's soft voice asked. "I just caught the news. Please tell me that wasn't your flight that made the emergency landing."

"Actually, it was."

"My god, what happened? Is everyone okay? Shelly?"

Joe heard the sudden fear in her voice. "Yes, we're fine. Everyone is fine. That's why I'm calling. Look, Teresa, I need you to come down here to Florida right away."

"You just said everyone is --"

"We're good, but there's something else, something you need to check out."

"Joe, you know I can't. Gary and I are catching a plane to Bermuda in the morning."

"Oh, right!" Joe muttered under his breath. "Your wedding anniversary. I'm sorry, I completely forgot."

"What's going on down there, Joe? What happened on the plane?"

"Shelly's all right, really," he said, predicting Teresa's instinct to care for and protect his daughter. "But she's worked up about something. Something she said happened on the plane."

"What? My god, did she do something on the plane to cause the emergency?" Teresa words came out fast and Joe heard the panic rise in her voice.

"No, no, she swears she did nothing, but there's something else." Joe hesitated, "There's a woman I think we need to see. I know, I know, she's not a child, but Shelly picked up on something."

"Well, can't you go and talk to her?"

"This isn't my thing."

After a long pause, Teresa replied, "Joe, if you think it's that urgent, I'll cancel our plans and come down. But this trip is very important to Gary and me. You know how much we've looked forward to it and how hard it was to plan for it."

"No, you're right," Joe conceded, "Don't cancel your trip. We don't even know for sure if there really is anything."

Teresa was the expert and Joe was uncomfortable having to make this assessment alone.

"Joe, you can do this," Teresa said encouragingly. "You said she's not a child and you know how to spot a fraud. Just look for the tricks. You'll be able to tell. I don't expect there are any more "trues" or even "carries" out there that we haven't already found and placed. It's extremely unlikely that we've missed one," she finished confidently.

"This one's different. She's not clairvoyant or telekinetic. She appears to have been in two places at the same time."

"Are you talking about bi-location? Remote Viewing?

'Yes, well, sort of," Joe replied.

"If I remember correctly, when the CIA and Department of Defense employed psychics to gather intelligence information, no women were used in those experiments. Anyway, they ended the program concluding the project didn't provide any useful information. We knew about their people. Not one of them was pure."

"Shelly insists she saw this woman on the plane with us and the news placed her at a school in Sarasota at the same time."

Teresa paused. "Sounds strange …*definitely* worth checking into."

"I'll go see her tomorrow- if I can. She's in a hospital south of here. I'll have to get to her quickly. The press already has coverage of the story," he said, thinking out loud.

"All right then. You go see her tomorrow. Make the assessment and if you find it necessary, send her up here the second she's able to travel. Impress upon her the need to be discrete. You can handle this one, Joe." Teresa said encouragingly. "I'll get back soon and I'll speak with her if you send her up." Teresa paused as another thought crossed her mind, "Remember, Joe, if this was a public 'reveal' then we may not be the only ones interested. Be very careful."

"I know," he agreed. "Have a good trip and say 'hello' to Gary for me."

The Emergency Room physician gently removed the bandages applied by the EMT from the still unconscious Christine, exposing a small hole above her left pelvic bone. He carefully probed the entrance wound, removed the bullet, and applied several tight stitches, then covered the wound with a large adhesive bandage.

The Neuro consult suggested a CAT scan to check for possible intra-cerebral hemorrhage caused by the fall and evidenced by the bump on her head. Fortunately, an hour later the scan came back showing no sign of internal bleeding. Christine was transferred to an empty semi-private room on the second floor of the trauma center and observed in ICU for the night.

The nurses in the ICU noticed that the young detective who took custody of the bullet was visibly irritated that he was not able to interview the victim.

"Any idea when she'll come around?" he gruffly asked a heavyset nurse.

"No telling with these kinds of injuries," she curtly replied back.

The detective reached into the breast pocket of his crisp uniform and produced a neat stack of cards held together with a thin blue rubber band.

"Well," he mumbled, "I can't wait around here all day." Wrestling a card out, he placed it on the countertop of the nurses' station. "Here's my number. Contact me as soon as she's able to communicate." Carelessly abandoning his empty cup of coffee next to his card, he hurried towards the elevators.

"Joe, aren't you worried about your cholesterol?" Rita asked over her black coffee and dry bagel.

Digging into his plate of scrambled eggs with a mountain of bacon piled on top of it, Joe replied curtly, "Cholesterol's not my problem."

Rita realized she'd put her foot in her mouth too late and quickly diverted conversation.

"Shelly seems to be taking the whole episode in stride," she said.

Joe looked up over Rita's shoulder. He could see Shelly already had half of a red grapefruit on her tray and was patiently waiting in the breakfast buffet line for a Belgian waffle.

"She's a tough one," he replied.

When Shelly sat down, the conversation changed to the Disney trip.

When it was time for Joe to leave, Shelly jumped up and hugged her father.

"You promise you'll go, right dad? You promise?" Shelly whispered in his ear, as she hugged him.

"Yes, Shelly, I'll go to the hospital today. I'll see your lady," he reassured her. He noticed the relief in Shelly's eyes.

"I love you honey, be good and have a great time," he said as he kissed her cheek.

"I love you too, daddy," she said and gave him one more big hug before she sat down to finish her breakfast.

"Rita, take good care of my girl, you know I trust you. Keep her safe," Joe said, giving Rita a hug.

"You know I will, Joe. Take care of yourself and don't worry. We're going to have a great time!" she reassured him.

Joe walked out to the parking lot and located the Avis sedan he had signed for before breakfast. He started towards the silver rental but decided to steal a moment in the bright, warm Florida sun.

His hands in his pockets, he wandered across the parking lot to a small pond. The sun was warm on his face and he was surprised by how bright it was. He reached into his shirt pocket and pulled out his favorite pair of *Ray Bans*, flicked them open and popped them on his face in one fluid motion. Gentle, dry winds blew over his skin and swept his thick curly hair across his forehead.

He was a little bit irritated that he would have to handle this unanticipated assignment. Teresa was able to spot a fraud a mile away and she was unsurpassed in her abilities and her dedication to her work in Research and Training. He realized, however, that she'd worked intensely for quite some time now so that she could take this trip. She needed a short break too.

Quietly, he stood and watched a fluffy white bird with a long, snakelike neck patiently study something in the grass with great intensity. Its beady eyes starred down its yellow beak as if it were a double barrel shotgun. Then, with impressive speed, the bird stabbed and consumed the prey. It was a swift and successful mission. Its patience and perseverance paid off, Joe mused.

He could do this. Joe got into the car and headed for the hospital to see the woman who was on the news last night. She may well be in danger. If Shelly was right, he needed to get this woman away before someone else realizes what he and Teresa had already suspected.

CHAPTER 7❀

Brenda Collins, a school reporter, had been on the local paper for only a short time but hoped to quickly advance into the major stories. She'd worked hard and did her homework. Discovering that Christine had no family in town, she posed as a relative from out of town and was easily admitted into the room.

She was waiting bedside when Christine regained consciousness.

A guttural groan emerged as Christine shuffled under the sheets and gradually opened her eyes. Focus came slowly through dry eyes and she was disoriented.

Brenda waited patiently like a lion waiting for its pray to come out of the brush and into the open.

"Ahh, awe," Christine moaned, her mouth dry and throat scratchy. "Where am I? Who are you?"

Avoiding one question, Brenda answered the other.

"You're in the hospital." Brenda covertly reached under the sweater folded on her lap and clicked on her tape recorder. "Do you remember what happened yesterday?"

"In the hospital?" Christine questioned as she tried to push down with her arms to sit up in the bed. "Ahh, no, I don't remember." Reaching down and feeling the bandages, she said, "My side hurts. What happened?"

"You don't remember *anything*? Try to think. You were at school yesterday morning," Brenda pressed, leaning in closer. "Do you remember yesterday morning?"

"No, I don't remember anything. My side! What happened?"

"You were shot in the hallway of Corwin Middle. You were unconscious and they took you here to Sarasota Memorial," Brenda offered, hoping to stir Christine's memory. "Do you know how it happened? Did you see who did it?"

"What? I was *shot*?" Christine said incredulously. "No! I don't remember anything at all!"

"Must be that bump on your head..." Disappointed that she wasn't going to make any progress with this woman who can't or won't remember, Brenda handed her a card. "If you remember anything, here's my number, please call me."

Confused, Christine looked at the card.

"You're a reporter?"

Brenda got up to leave when Christine asked, "Can you tell *me* what happened? I can't remember. Was anyone else hurt? "

"No. No one else was injured," Brenda quickly told her. "At the press conference the police told us that there was a shooting at your school, and the school went into lock down. An employee, that would be you, was shot in the hallway and rushed to the hospital. No one could come on campus for most of the day. You can imagine the parents and reporters trying to gain entrance onto campus. We were detained in the teacher's lounge…"

"..the children! Are the children okay?" Christine interrupted.

"They're all fine," Brenda consoled. "Once the campus was searched and secured, the students were released to their parents. Buses were called in to transport any remaining students home." She paused while Christine took it all in. Giving her one last chance to remember she added, "Are you *sure* you don't know what happened or who shot you?"

"I wish I could, but I just can't remember."

Upon hearing voices, two nurses rushed into the room.

"Contact that investigator and let him know the patient is conscious," a round nurse in a busy and vibrantly colored uniform told the younger nurse.

"Call me if you remember anything." Brenda whispered to Christine and then she slipped past the nurse and out of the room.

The heavyset nurse waddled over to Christine and checked the equipment recording her vital signs.

"What happened…"

"Hush, now, relax for a moment and let me check your blood pressure," the nurse said. "Would you like some water?"

"Yes, I'm really thirsty, and my side hurts. What happened to me?"

"Now, now, just relax there Sugar," the nurse said condescendingly. "You need to stay still. I'll give you a little more pain medicine and you'll feel much better." She adjusted a little valve on the tube increasing the drip from the bag into the IV, and then to Christine's dismay, quickly left the room.

A little while later, Christine heard voices outside her room. She recognized Brenda's voice and a man's voice. Suddenly, another female voice entered into the conversation and immediately Christine's stomach tightened into a knot.

A moment later, into the room sauntered a young detective. Although more persistent than Brenda, Christine was still unable to answer and apologized that she had no memory of what had occurred. The detective pulled out another card from the rubber banded stack in his pocket and set it on her hospital table next to the plastic water pitcher, asking her to call him immediately if she remembered anything.

As soon as he left the room, she heard him speak again to someone, and then to her alarm, in walked the other woman whose voice she'd recognized in the hallway.

It was Martha.

"I met your reporter in the hall. What did you tell her?"

Thanks for your concern, Martha; I'm in a lot of pain right now, how are you, Christine sarcastically thought to herself.

"I didn't tell her anything. I don't remember anything," Christine snapped in response to Martha's blatant inconsideration.

"The principal explicitly told all of us not to speak to the press. They're making a mess of the school's reputation," Martha said, hovering over Christine. "My school had to close today because of you. And likely again tomorrow, possibly even the rest of the week. Reporters are crawling all over campus and making it impossible for the rest of us to do our jobs.

"Until they find out who it was that came on campus or how you managed to get yourself shot, we all have to stay low key. You must tell the police who it was right away so they can stop poking around the school and leave the rest of us alone."

"I just told you, I don't remember anything."

"I am hiring a replacement for you immediately." Martha's words spilled out of her mouth. "Then, after all of this is all cleared up, perhaps we can discuss a possible return."

"What? I'm being fired?!" Christine cried in disbelief.

"Take some time off, Christine," Martha said, feigning concern. "You may not feel comfortable returning to the school. And don't talk to the press," she added. "You'll only create more trouble for yourself and the school."

With that, the Mantis turned and, following her nose, slithered out of the room.

CHAPTER 8❀

Joe already felt guilty about stealing the stethoscope from a nurse's station so when he saw the officer leave Christine's room, his heart nearly stopped.

The officer paused to speak to two women then one of them went into Christine's room and the other left. Once the officer passed him, Joe breathed a sigh of relief and waited for the dark haired woman who was speaking very aggressively to leave the room.

Joe entered the room and recognized Christine immediately.

"Hello," Joe said cautiously, eyeing her curiously.

Christine looked at the tall, exceptionally handsome stranger and she felt a weak flutter rise up into her throat. She felt her face warm as blood flushed into her cheeks.

"Are you Christine Smith?"

"Yes?" She starred at him, unable to tear her eyes from his face. The attraction to him was immediate; visceral. Something about him was so familiar. Had she seen him somewhere before, she wondered?

Joe pulled up a chair.

"My name's Joe Pasquali and I have a very strange question to ask you."

Noticing the stethoscope, Christine stammered, "Hi, Dr. Pasquali, are you my doctor?"

She was struggling to sit up just a little bit straighter and was suddenly very concerned about the way she looked. However, her discomfort was quickly replaced by suspicion when he hesitated to answer.

"Are you another reporter? I've already told everyone I don't remember what happened. And I've been *told* not to talk to reporters- bad for the school and all," Christine said, resentfully. Feeling childish, she wished she did remember something, right now, so she could tell him, if only to spite Martha.

"I'm not a reporter and I'm sorry, I'm not a doctor either. But I had to see you- please, if you'll let me explain..." he implored.

Christine was torn between irritation and fascination with this man. She was surprised that she felt this instant attraction. He really wasn't her type at all. Her past boyfriends were average height and she preferred them to have dark hair. Joe's sandy colored hair went perfectly with his hazel eyes and he was at least six feet tall. Yet his presence felt so familiar. She wasn't about to dismiss him away.

"Yesterday my daughter and I were on a plane going to Orlando. My daughter is convinced," he chuckled nervously, "that you were on the plane with us." *There, straight to the point*, he thought and watched Christine's face closely. He recognized her all right, but there was something else….

Christine starred at him.

"What? A plane?" Her eyes crinkled slightly with amusement, but then suddenly her heart started racing. *"A plane?"* The words echoed in her head. Her grin quickly vanished, replaced by terror as flecks of memory from the previous day came crashing back into her conscience like tiny meteors.

"What's happening?" Her eyes darted around the hospital room. "The plane…the girl…ooh, my side!" Her mind recalled the entire event instantly. Christine reached down and put both hands on the bandages on her side. She looked up at Joe, her eyes pleading.

Joe was equally surprised and concerned to see her face so quickly change to shock.

"You remember being on the plane?" He studied her face intently. "What did she look like, the girl? What did she look like?"

Now, without any hesitation, Christine answered. "Blond wavy hair, blue eyes…"

Reaching into his chino's pants pocket Joe pulled out his wallet, took out a picture of Shelly, and handed it to Christine.

"Is this her? Did you see my daughter?"

"Oh, my God. That's her! That's the girl at the school…" Christine looked around the room quickly as if she didn't know where she was, then locked eyes with Joe "...on a plane!"

They stared at one another for a moment waiting for the other to speak.

Christine suddenly lurched upright; pain searing into her side. "Is she alright?" she cried.

"Yes! Shelly's fine. Somehow... thanks to you... I think." Joe stammered.

Relaxing a bit, Christine sputtered, "What... how did this happen?"

Joe wondered how much he should tell her. He could see she was alarmed and distressed. He definitely knew Teresa would want to see her.

Joe needed to prepare Christine for what she was about to hear. Somehow she had connected with his daughter, possibly even saved her. But he wasn't good at this kind of thing. It was Teresa's area of expertise.

He took a deep breath and began. "Miss Smith....?"

"Call me Chris." She had always been called Christine. She never liked the short nick name. She wondered why she'd said that!

"Chris, if what we think happened, happened, you can't tell anyone that you remember. It won't be long before the report comes back on the bullet they removed from you. They will eventually realize they have a match to the gun used on the plane. And they'll come down hard on you. How will you explain this to them?"

"I can't! I really don't know how it happened! I couldn't have been there- I wasn't on the plane... only in my mind- I was at the school!" Christine was starting to spiral in confusion and panic.

"Do you know what will happen if other people find out? There are people who will insist that you remember and demand to know how you did it,"

Joe said honestly. "Chris, I'm afraid you are going to be in grave danger."

Christine considered him for a moment as fear welled up inside of her. *What was he saying?*

"What kind of people?"

Joe paused, wondering how to tell her without alarming her even more.

"Chris, do you believe in Psychics or Mediums?"

"What kind of a question is that?" she asked. "No, I don't."

"Why not?"

"It's luck. Just plain old lucky guesses. Coincidence. It happens to me all the time. And I'm not a psychic or a mind reader," she said, indignantly.

Joe considered this "tell" of information.

"What if it isn't luck?"

"Well, I still don't believe because no one can tell the future. If someone could, they'd be playing the lottery every week and winning! Why would you ask me that?"

Joe persisted, leading her down the path.

"What would happen if someone did win the lottery every week?"

"Well, they would probably have lots of people wanting to borrow money from them, maybe wanting to know *how* they…!"

Christine suddenly realized that Joe was right. She could be in danger. She knew she wasn't crazy. They'd be sure to connect the bullet and the gun soon and come after her for answers, just like Joe said.

"My god, what am I going to do?"

"There's a place in New Jersey called MIRC…."

"What? Wait! I know that place!" Christine interrupted incredulously. "The Medical Intensive Recovery Center."

Joe did not correct her.

"We can take care of you there," he jumped in. "You need to get out of here and go where you'll be safe. I can arrange for all of your travel," Joe said. "You should leave as soon as you are able!"

CHAPTER 9 ❀

Pressing her cheek against the stinging cold window of the MIRC limo, Christine winced as she squirmed against the door. Her pain medication was wearing off quickly and she was having a difficult time finding a comfortable position. Her side was throbbing and she knew from the dampness that the bandages needed to be changed. The limo was inundated with hot, parched air, adding to her discomfort.

"Do you think you could please turn down the heat a little?" she asked the uniformed driver.

A large metal sign announced the arrival to the small town:

Packton- Population 2005. Incorporated 1912.

Christine's anxiety began to grow as they drove past the park, the church, and the small row of stores.

A surreal feeling came over her as she vaguely recognized the once familiar landmarks of this antiquated town.

A crusty pile of gravel pitted snow mounded up against the curb. The driver slowed down and cautiously pulled over.

"Is this the place?" the driver asked.

Christine shuffled closer against the door. She erased more of the fog around the thawed smear left by her cheek, enlarging the portal, and looked out.

Through the encroaching dusk and though it had been many years, she clearly recognized the little house. It had been repainted the palest of yellows, and yet, to her, stood out boldly against the dimming snow engulfing it. It looked dwarfed beneath the trees around it, which had grown much taller. Snow sat thickly in the elbows of their bare branches as they reached for the pasty gray sky.

A new garage replaced the old red barn, and a large wooden play set stood where the old chicken coop used to be.

"Thank you," she said. Nostalgia crept in and overwhelmed her. She choked back a sob and wiped away the tear running down her cheek. "We can leave now."

The driver slowly pulled away from the curb.

"Was that your house?" he asked, peering at her through the rear view mirror.

"No, it was my grandmother's. My father and uncle were raised there. It was sold after my grandmother died. I haven't been back since."

"Never thought you'd be coming back to this town, huh?"

"This town? No. Never."

She painfully remembered how the children in this town had treated her. They were incredibly mean. And although she loved to visit and take "secret missions" to explore the adjacent properties, the kids in town didn't like her or her grandmother very much.

They drove past the swiftly moving brook. Snow topped the rocks on either side of the water like round white toupees, and an occasional chip of ice floated along. She remembered how cold the spring water was, even in the middle of summer. Near the brook, on the other side of the ugly barbed wire fence, was a stand of naked lilac bushes, overgrown and barren of their abundant foliage and fragrant blooms.

Lilacs were Christine's favorite flowers. She missed them. Those lilac bushes used to belong to her grandmother until the neighbor's land was sold and a dispute arose over the property line. The lilacs that her grandmother so lovingly planted and cared for eventually had to be surrendered over.

She braced herself against the door as the driver cautiously navigated seven treacherous bumps in the road that lead to the main gate of the estate.

"Hold on. This is a rough climb," he warned.

"I know. Jacob's Ladder."

"Haven't heard it called that in a while," the driver said. "Always wondered where that name came from."

"My grandmother told me why. That according to a Biblical story, a man named Jacob dreamt of a ladder that reached down to earth from heaven so that the angels could go back and forth."

"Unlikely that MIRC wanted anyone to *go back and forth*," he replied, obviously amused by the legend.

He's right, Christine thought, noting the abundance of *No Trespassing* signs scattered all over the property.

"I used to walk my bike up to the top. It was a great ride coming back down!" She recalled, as she tolerated the increasing pain from each of the seven jolts.

Not the ladder, nor the loosely locked gates, or even her grandmother's stern warnings not to trespass on *that* property ever stopped her from hiking or biking up the hill to explore. It was exciting to investigate this concealed estate with its ancient statues and pools.

Besides, that's where she found her refuge.

The driver finally turned left and approached the main gate.

The entrance was exactly as she remembered. On each side of the huge wrought iron gates, high cement walls with matching lion heads stood. Her grandmother herself had played on the property as a child and had told her that many decades earlier water had flowed from the lions' mouths down into large reflection pools below. Christine could see the rust on the gates and the chipped, cracked concrete of the pool and lion heads under the layers of snow. A few inches of black, sludgy water, thickly tinged with soft white snow sat in the reflection pools below.

A newer, larger, more alarming sign caught her eye.

TRESPASSERS WILL BE PROSECUTED

The driver rolled down his window and a dry, frigid air flowed into the limo. The rusty old gates now held an electric sensor and a keypad to restrict access and he punched a series of numbers onto the keypad.

The tightly clenched teeth of the gates slowly yawned open.

She studied the fading, shadowy landscape amazed that she was back in this place that time forgot; now trying herself to be forgotten.

The Medical Intensive Recovery Center was expecting her. MIRC, she remembered, was a mansion and private convalescent manor for the "rich and famous" requiring complete seclusion.

She recalled the town kids used to try to scare her by retelling rumors about MIRC's secret history and the rich Italian family that had built it.

Joe promised her that she would get the protection she needed and the physical care she required and that she would be safe at MIRC. Something about him made her trust him. She believed him. And besides, what other choice did she have?

He seemed confident that if she was removed immediately from public view, the attention would pass and that most people would forget what had happened.

"With any luck," he'd said, "only a few people on the plane, at the school and in the hospital, will still speculate."

Regretting that he would be out of the country when she arrived at MIRC, he promised to see her there soon.

"In the meantime, and most importantly," he assured her, "you'll receive excellent medical care and privacy."

Christine knew that her life had changed forever. She wasn't sure what had happened to her, but it seemed MIRC was her only option at this point. She had come here to hide, to escape, from the reporters and the police and all of the questions they would soon have.

It was dark when the limo pulled up to the east wing. A shiver ran down her spine when all of a sudden her grandmother's stern warning echoed in her head.

"Stay 'way from them, Christina. Don't you neva disturb *them people*."

CHAPTER 10 ❀

A woman in a long heavy brown coat with a white knit scarf over her head and around her neck was standing at the end of the sidewalk with a wheelchair.

"How are the roads, George?" Christine heard the woman ask the driver when he got out of the Limo. The driver went around the limo and opened the door to help Christine get into the wheelchair.

"Pretty slick, but I got her here in one piece," he said as he took Christine's arm and eased her into the chair.

A heavy woolen blanket was draped over the chair and the woman and the driver worked together to pull it over and around Christine to keep her warm.

"Hello, Christine. I'm Maxine. I'll be taking care of you. Let's get you to your room before you catch your death of cold," she said, shivering.

"I think my bandages need to be changed," Christine said, feeling the warm dampness on her side suddenly turn cold.

"Yes, dear, I'll take care of that right away."

"And I'm due for some pain medication, I left the hospital so fast, I didn't get any to take with me...."

"Don't worry about a thing," Maxine assured her as she wheeled her down the bumpy cobblestone path around the side of the building and into the dimly lit, diminutive, aesthetic room. "We're going to take good care of you."

Maxine helped Christine into the small gurney-type bed and swiftly changed the dressing then gave her a painkilling injection in her arm.

Exhausted from the trip, and having just been given medication, Christine fell quickly to sleep. She disassociated from the cold, stiff sheet, the hushed voices down the hallway, and the smell of rubbing alcohol. The last image in her mind was the recent sight of the lilac bushes. The harsh, cold winter had stripped and exposed them leaving behind no hint of their beauty.

Before she fell into the emerging dream state, she recalled an earlier memory when the bushes were laden and bursting with life and of a summer day when she had struggled to pull out a large, heavy rock from the brook. It was smooth and flat on one side and had made a perfect seat. She was warmed by the dappled sunlight, sitting there under the umbrella of the fragrant lilac bushes. The trickling water and the heart shaped leaves and fragrant purple blossoms surrounded her as she sat in her secret and safe hiding place.

Then suddenly the memory went dark and a very different dream emerged.

She was in a bedroom at her grandmother's house. It was a hot, sultry night. A street lamp dimly lit the room. She was standing in front of the window looking down at the brook. The window was open and instead of heavy perfumed air from the lilacs wafting up into the tiny room, the smell of old and decaying vegetation encased her. Her body was naked and damp and covered with wet mud.

On the cot at MIRC, Christine was sweating. A fever had set in during the night.

It was early in the morning when Christine woke up and heard muffled voices and opened her eyes to the soft glow of florescent lighting entering her dark room from the hallway. She heard a door creak open down the corridor, followed by footsteps.

"Christine, it's me," Maxine announced, anticipating Christine's apprehension.

A few more footsteps and the nurse rounded the corner and came into the room. It was the woman from the night before. She was dressed in a stiff, starched, white dress, white sneakers, and white pantyhose that went "swish, swish" as she crossed the room to the small window. She opened the crisp, Wedgwood blue and white curtains allowing sunlight to flood into the tiny room.

In the early morning light Christine was able to get a better look at her. Christine thought she was old for a nurse, in her late sixties, and her bright pink lipstick looked very much out of place against her pasty white skin. Her thin gray hair was pinned up with silver bobby pins into a loose, old-fashioned beehive that looked like a thick spider web sitting on top of her head.

"Good morning, Christine. I'm Maxine, You probably don't remember meeting me from last night. How are you feeling this morning?" Maxine chattered as she set down a tray holding a glass of water and a mini paper cup with one large white and two little yellow pills.

"I guess I'm ok. I'm feeling wet."

"I'm sorry. We'll get you taken care of." Maxine took a thermometer out of her pocket, shook it and popped it into Christine's mouth. "Your side should start to feel less tender. I'll be especially careful when I change your dressing this morning." Maxine soothingly replied, as she took the thermometer back and raised an eyebrow when she saw the reading. She handed over the glass and pills.

Christine took all three pills together and washed them down with water, handing the glass back.

"What are the all the pills for?" she asked.

"One is for your pain and the others are antibiotics. You ran a pretty high fever last night, that's why you're all sweaty."

"Yeah, I don't feel great this morning. Will a pill be strong enough for my pain?" Christine asked. She was getting used to the instant effects of an IV or injection.

"We need to start to wean you off the pain medications. These should work nearly as well, although they may take a bit longer to start working.

Let me know if the pain grows intolerable, we can give you a second pain pill."

Christine laid back and gingerly rolled onto her right side and watched Maxine gather the supplies necessary to change the dressing on the wound just above Christine's left hip.

Maxine went over to a small sink surrounded by a built-in unit on the wall in front of her bed and ran warm water into a pan. She reached up into a cabinet above the sink and collected a neatly folded white towel and washcloth from the stack inside the cabinet and laid them and the pan of water on the table next to Christine's bed.

"What's that in the corner?" Christine asked, noticing a stand with a monitor on it with lots of wires hanging down. It was the only piece of medical equipment visible in the tiny room.

"That's a sleep monitor."

Maxine reached into another drawer near the sink and got out some clean gauze, pads, and bandages and carried them over to the same table.

"What's it for?"

"They are particularly useful when we have someone…." Maxine hesitated as she chose her words carefully, "…. experiencing sleep problems."

Then Maxine said calmly, "Okay, Christine, I know this is the worst part, so hang in there."

Christine braced herself and tightened her hold on the bed rail.

"Yeah, I know."

With gloved hands, Maxine carefully unwrapped the ace bandage that was drawn across Christine's midsection. Christine raised her back and side up off the bed so Maxine could get around her.

When the pressure from the bandage was released Christine recoiled slightly as the pain intensified briefly and finally passed. Christine carefully returned back onto her side position, sinking in against the two pillows.

"Ready?" Maxine asked.

"Yeah, go ahead," Christine replied thru clenched teeth and grabbed onto the bed's railing once again for support.

Last night Maxine had applied a larger than usual piece of gauze to cover more than just the wound, so that when it was removed she would not be pushing over the swelling. She picked at a weak corner of the first-aid tape with her bony fingers and carefully pulled it back, pushing down against the skin with her free hand and examined the wound briefly. It was red and irritated and still swollen but did not appear to be very infected.

This girl was lucky, it could have been much worse, Maxine thought to herself as she squeezed out the wash cloth and dabbed and cleaned around the inside of the wound, working outward, rinsing often. If all goes well the stitches could be removed in another day, two perhaps. Even though she didn't like to do doctor's work, she would remove the stitches herself, knowing that this patient required complete confidentiality. She quickly applied dry gauze, taping it on with first-aid tape, and wrapped the elastic bandage around Christine's torso, making two complete passes around her lower midsection.

When she was done, Christine watched as Maxine collected all of the soiled gauze and bandages and disposed of them in a little garbage can in the corner of the room that was lined with thick red plastic. Christine caught a glimpse of the bandage Maxine was discarding, and noticed that there was much less blood and that the gauze was free of yellow or green pus.

"Thank you, Maxine," Christine said as she melted back into the pillows behind her on the bed. "Didn't feel a thing," Christine said, rolling her eyes away.

Ignoring the sarcasm, Maxine replied, "It looks good. A little red but it's healing and I promise the swelling *will* go down soon. I'll be taking those stitches out for you soon," Maxine said as she finished washing her hands at the sink.

"Wait, isn't a doctor supposed to remove stitches?"

"Honey, I've been a nurse longer than you are old! I've taken care of a lot worse, and the only time we need a *real* doctor up here is when there is a life-threatening emergency, which thankfully, in all my years here, has never happened once."

Uh oh. What have I gotten into, Christine thought. *Medical Intensive Recovery Center and no doctors in this place?* Christine wondered if she'd made the right decision by coming here.

"How long have you worked at MIRC?" Christine asked her to try to get a better feel for who this woman was. She was surprised that Maxine hadn't asked her anything about the incident.

Maxine was trained to never expose MIRC and patient confidentialities, but she rarely had an opportunity to talk about herself. No patient every really asked her.

"I've lived in this town my whole life. Started working as a nurse for the local hospital outside of town. I didn't like the institutional environment of a large hospital so I went into private nursing for a family on the other side of the hill. But when MIRC offered me an opportunity here - I couldn't refuse- been here ever since."

MIRC was sounding more like an institution of sorts, not quite a hospital.

Now it was Maxine's turn to change the subject.

"Are you ready for some breakfast?"

"I'm not very hungry now, but could I have some coffee? I'm not used to this cold weather anymore. Something hot would be great," Christine replied.

"I'll be right back with hot coffee," Maxine said as she headed out the door and down the corridor.

Christine waited until she heard the door open and close behind Maxine at the end of the hall. In the quiet she let out a long sigh, mulling over Maxine's revelation.

A medical center with no doctors?

CHAPTER 11 ❁

While she waited for Maxine to return, Christine relaxed into the pillows on her right side and glanced at the clock on the table beside the bed. It was nearly 8:30 am. On any other day, she would be driving to work now. She had loved her job at the school but knew she could never go back there again. She was sure that Martha had poisoned Principal Holston with lies about her. According to Martha, the employees at the school wanted to avoid bad press and the principal was irritated by the coverage. And it seemed, somehow, it was all Christine's fault.

Christine never got close to many people in her life, and it made her sad that the only one from the school who came to see her was Martha. And who knew what Martha had been telling others. Even though she wasn't there, Christine could feel a river of curiosity, fear, and speculation growing as her co-workers must be wondering what had happened. Now, instead of talking incessantly about her prize-winning orchids, Christine knew Martha would be gossiping about her.

Christine's ears warmed and her cheeks burned with frustration and anger. She was forced to write off that short Florida chapter of her life. She could never go back there now, even if she wanted to.

She turned her attention toward the tiny window facing the east. She watched as the sun shone brighter outside, the trees casting shadows on the hills beyond the building.

A few minutes later she heard the door down the hall open again and quickly recognized the padded footsteps of Maxine. Christine had very acute hearing. She was a careful listener; always alert and able to identify sounds.

Maxine entered the brightening room balancing a tray containing a stainless steel carafe, a white linen napkin, a teaspoon, and a small silver cream and sugar set. There was also a brightly painted porcelain teacup and saucer and an oversized lemon poppy seed muffin sat on a matching floral plate.

"I thought when you *do* get hungry, you might like to nibble on something," Maxine said as she placed the collection down next to the clock on the adjustable table near Christine's bed.

Maxine turned to Christine, studying her demeanor.

"Thanks," Christine said, realizing that she was hungry after all.

"Joe said I would be meeting with Mrs. Darby when I got here. Am I scheduled to meet with her today, do you know?" Christine asked.

"Yes, actually, sometime later on Teresa will be dropping by to see you. You'll like her. She is very sweet. She's been working at MIRC for quite some time now and she is doing excellent work."

Christine thought that was an unusual phrase. *Doing excellent work? What does that mean?*

"Joe didn't tell me much about her. Is she a psychiatrist?" Christine asked pensively.

Maxine walked around to the other side of the bed.

"No, actually she's Director of Research and Training *and* a very good listener," she replied, handing the TV remote to Christine.

"Here's the remote if you would like to watch some TV. Can I get you anything else right now?" Maxine asked calmly.

"No thank you. I think I have everything I need for now," Christine answered.

Christine pointed the remote at the TV hanging in the corner of the room and pressed the "power on" button. The Weather Channel immediately appeared on the screen.

"…and later this evening, New Jersey is in for even more snow…"

Looking towards the window once again, Christine noticed heavy gray clouds lingering above the hillside.

CHAPTER 12 ✿

At eleven o'clock the door opened down the hall and Christine heard the clip-clip of heels on the marble floors. A knock on her open door echoed in the empty hallway.

"Yes? Come in," Christine said.

A petite woman in her middle forties, dressed in a neat and tailored dark salmon colored pantsuit with a white blouse entered and walked over to Christine's bed.

"Hello, Christine. I'm Teresa Darby," she said, extending her right hand out to Christine.

Christine returned the firm handshake with a much less confident one.

"You're the one Joe told me about. He said you'd be able to tell me what happened to me."

"How are you feeling?" Teresa's tiny blue eyes shimmered like crystals floating within the milky white skin of her face. She dressed very simply. The only jewelry she wore was a white gold wedding band with matching diamond engagement ring.

"I'm feeling better."

"Are you feeling well enough for us to take a little walk? If you're up to it, would you like to go into the main house? There's a pretty solarium there."

Having only heard about but never seen the inside of the mansion, Christine was unable to contain her excitement.

"I'd love to see the house! Yes, I think I can make it, but I'm pretty slow."

"Not a problem. Take your time."

Christine managed to steady herself on the edge of the bed and carefully stood up.

"Can I help you in any way?" Teresa extended her arm out for support.

Christine took a moment to get her balance. "No, I'm good."

Slightly bent and holding her side, Christine slowly entered a hallway outside of her room.

She could tell that this area was just an extension of the old mansion. A wooden closet door was between her and the double doors on her left that lead to the main house. To her right was the door to the outside that she had been brought in through on her arrival.

As they passed through the double doors, it felt to Christine that everything had suddenly changed.

The sharp, medicinal smell of the small wing was replaced by the odors of aged tapestries on the walls, musty antiqued chairs with their faded burgundy upholstery, all mixing with the earthy scent of thick wood moldings.

Christine squinted as her eyes also had to adjust. The florescent glow of the small hallway was suddenly replaced by fresh, brilliant light flooding into the enormous parlor through several large stained glass windows high above.

Even the air on her skin felt different.

Teresa led Christine through another set of double doors on their right into a small sitting room. The dazzling white snow outside was framed by a wall of tall windows. Flanking the doorway on both sides were built-in bookcases overcrowded with books. A black, white and burgundy colored oriental carpet sat on top of a dark slate floor. Four overstuffed white chairs encircled a round glass coffee table the in middle of the room, forming a cozy sitting area

Teresa helped Christine settle into one of the chairs.

"What an amazing place this is! I've always wondered what the inside looked like."

"How is it that you've heard about us?"

"My grandmother…"

Suddenly Christine was startled by a knock on the double doors behind her.

"It's Maxine, Christine." Teresa was facing the doors and motioned Maxine in.

"I thought I'd find you two here," Maxine said as she entered the room. "It's time for your medicine, Christine." Carrying a glass of water in one hand and small paper cup in the other, she handed them to Christine. "Teresa, may I get anything for you?"

"No. Thank you very much, Maxine."

Teresa turned her attention back to Christine. "How did you say you knew about us?"

Christine swallowed the pills with the water and handed the glass back to Maxine. Maxine turned and started to leave the room, calling over her shoulder, "Lunch will be ready soon."

"My grandmother lived in the house at the bottom of the hill," Christine answered proudly, "Tina Smith."

Teresa could not help but notice Maxine's back stiffen and her purposeful hesitation before she stepped through the archway and slowly closed the doors behind her.

"Tina Smith? Hum, was your grandfather William?"

"Yes. How'd you know? Have you also lived here all of your life like Maxine?"

"No, but I do know a bit about the town and its history. Let's see. Smith…Smith…Two boys? Your father and his brother, right?"

"Yes. My father's name was Anthony and my uncle is David."

"Your father's name *was*?"

"I don't remember much about him. He died when I was a little girl."

"I'm sorry. And you didn't have any brothers or sisters?"

"No. Just my mom and me, and grandma. Oh, I have some cousins from Uncle David if that counts, but I haven't seen them for many years. We moved away and lost touch."

"I see. When was the last time you were in Packton?"

"Not since I was a kid."

"So you are familiar with MIRC?" Teresa's asked, raising one eyebrow. "Had you been up here before?"

"Not up to the mansion. I knew it was here, but it was too thickly hidden. But sometimes I would hide on the property to get away from the other kids who lived here. I knew they wouldn't follow me through the gates."

"Why did you think they wouldn't follow you onto the property?"

"They were afraid."

"Afraid of what?"

"They were always telling ghost stories about this place and making stuff up about the family who used to live here."

"I see. And you weren't afraid?"

"No, I knew this was the only place they wouldn't chase me and I'd be safe. I never believed the stories."

Teresa hesitated a moment then sat comfortably back in her chair and changed gears.

"O.k., so tell me what happened that put you in the hospital in Florida." She observed Christine shift uneasily in her chair.

"Well, one minute I was at the school in the hallway and then I was on a plane and then I woke up in the hospital!" Christine spouted. "You don't think I'm crazy...do you?" Christine asked directly, looking closely at Teresa's face. "I've thought about that, you know, that I might be crazy. But it was all real and it did all happen, so how does that make *me* crazy?"

"Slow down just a minute. Take a deep breath and relax. First of all, I do not think you are crazy.

Joe left me a message before he left Florida and I've done some research this morning. From what I've been able to put together, you are most certainly not crazy. And you obviously have evidence to the contrary."

Christine nodded in agreement, putting her hand over her injury and relaxed back in her chair, relief on her face.

"At first I thought yours was a case of Remote Viewing," Teresa explained.

"What's that?" Christine interrupted.

"The government tried experiments years ago where they asked psychics to see objects hidden in boxes. Then they tried to get the psychics to attempt to view a scene in a distant location."

"But I'm not psychic and I didn't just *see* something. I was really there. They took a bullet from my side. That's proof."

"Yes, I know. Those experiments were discontinued. It was concluded that the psychics used in the experiment were not true psychics. So, I did some more research and came upon a phenomenon called bi-location."

"Bi-location? What's that?"

"Another name for it is astral projection or projection of a double. This phenomenon dates back to ancient times. There has been little evidence of it in modern times. Saints, monks and holy people practiced being in two places at the same time. Padre Pio of Italy was said to have actually done this. And he is the only one who ever left evidence."

"What kind of evidence?" Christine asked, mouth agape and mesmerized by this new information.

"He visited a sick woman once and she asked him to leave proof of his visit. The bed sheet with the blood of his stigmatized hand print is on public display in Borgomanero, today."

"Whoa, so, that's what I did, I re-located?"

"*Bi*-located," Teresa corrected. "That's how it appears. Has anything like this ever happened to you before?"

"No! Nothing like this!" Christine put her hand over her bandaged side. "I always knew I was a little different. As a kid, I somehow *knew* things. I was teased a lot by the other kids and some of them were afraid of me. I tried to convince them that I was just lucky, that's all. I finally learned just not to tell. Then we moved and I had a chance to start over. But I never *did* anything to anyone!" Christine cried in alarm. "At least, I don't *think* I did."

A squeaky cart rolled towards them from the far end of the hallway. Maxine again appeared on the other side of the double glass doors and Teresa motioned her to enter. Maxine propped open the doors and pushed the cart into the room. On it were two white trays holding identical lunches- a bowl full of steaming red tomato soup and a butter toasted grilled cheese sandwich. A glass pitcher of water with lemons floating on the top was between the trays along with two crystal water glasses, cloth napkins and two soup spoons.

"I've brought lunch for you both. I thought Christine would much rather eat in here than in her room," announced Maxine to Teresa.

"That was thoughtful of you, Maxine. We are just about finished for today."

Teresa rose from her chair and walked over to a large wooden blanket rack on the far wall and brought a soft and lightweight quilt to Christine, laying it over her lap. "If you're comfortable, stay and eat. After lunch I recommend that you get some rest."

Without waiting for a response, Teresa addressed Maxine.

"Maxine, Christine can be moved to an upstairs bedroom this afternoon."

Maxine stared at Teresa. Their eyes locked for a moment as the implications of a new guest being brought into the manor was silently acknowledged between them.

Maxine hesitated to accept the directive and an awkward moment of silence ensued.

"I'll see that arrangements are made," Maxine said finally and left the room.

"I'm being moved?"

"You'll have a much nicer room where I hope you'll sleep better. The main house is run like a bed and breakfast, sort of. Three meals a day are provided; you won't want to be late downstairs for meals. Chef Diana likes her food eaten at the temperatures at which they are served. Speaking of which, go ahead and eat your lunch while it is still hot. We'll talk again tomorrow."

With that, Teresa left, leaving Christine alone and confused.

Teresa's untouched tray sat next to hers on the coffee table. She was surprised at how famished she was. The hardy scent of the soup made her stomach churn.

Her first bite of the toasted sandwich was interrupted by the faint giggling of children from out in the hallway behind her. Christine stiffened and the hair rose gently on the back of her neck.

CHAPTER 13 ✿

Christine returned to her room after eating every last bit of her lunch. She felt very tired, but proud that she had gotten back to her room without help. The main house was so quiet. She saw no sign of the children she swore she had heard earlier.

She went over to the small window in her room. The hills in the distance had a more amber hue than they had that morning, with the sun now on the other side of the mansion. She paused briefly to take in the splendor of the hillside and then closed the blinds.

Upon Teresa's advice she climbed into bed.

Christine succumbed peacefully to the medicated sleep surrounded by the quietness and seclusion of the hillside. Unfortunately, her comfort and security eventually gave way to disturbing dreams embedded with bits of childhood memories.

She was about ten years old and on the MIRC property. She was following a small stream exploring the creek banks and bottoms, finding large, smooth rocks then lifting them to see if she could catch a crayfish. She came upon three cement pools sitting on large pedestals, full of thick, black water from years of fallen leaves and debris.

Suddenly, the spring that fed the creek started to fill up the cracked pools with fresh water. The black sludge faded away, and the vines that seeped into the pools receded. It looked fresh and new, like she imagined it might have in her grandmother's day.

Then she heard whispers coming from the bushes behind her.

"Carmine, where are you?"

"Be quite Tina! I'm over here. Shhhh, here he comes!"

Out of the corner of her eye, Christine noticed movement near the gates. A round little boy with red hair and lots of freckles, about eight or nine years old, was slowly squeezing through the shiny black wrought iron gates.

A yell from the boy called Carmine in the bushes, suddenly startled her.

"NOW!"

Suddenly two children, a boy and a girl, jumped from their hiding places and pelted the red-haired boy with small round rocks.

In her dream, Christine instantly reacted. She ran over to the poor little boy to try to protect him.

"Stop it!" She cried out to the cruel children. She turned around to see if the red haired boy was hurt. He had blood on his cheek. When he saw her, his eyes widened with fear. He suddenly turned and ran away, crying.

Christine thought that she must have been hit by a rock also because her side started to hurt. She looked down and she was bleeding.

"Angie, you always ruin our fun!" giggled the girl.

"You won't tell mom, will you Angelina?" the boy asked Christine, his hands still full of rocks. "Angelina? Angeline..."

"..teen? Christine? " Maxine whispered into the room.

The dream blurred and faded swiftly as Christine woke up in the dark room. She rolled over and saw the florescent light from the hallway through the half open door of her room.

"Maxine, is that you? What time is it?"

"It's seven thirty. I checked on you several times around dinner, but you were fast asleep. You must have needed the rest."

"Wow, I had a really weird dream just before you came in."

"A dream?" Maxine asked with full attention. "You should let Teresa know about it. I'm sure she will find it very useful."

There's that word again... thought Christine. *...useful.*

"Oh, dear, was I supposed to be at dinner tonight? I hope the Chef wasn't mad." Christine asked, feeling badly she may have angered someone on her very first night.

"No, you're not expected for proper meals until tomorrow," Maxine said as she turned on a tubular light over the sink, shedding warm florescent light into the room. "Are you ready to move to your new room upstairs?"

"Yes, I think so."

"All right then. It's all ready for you." Maxine reached out to help Christine.

"I can do it myself now, thank you," Christine said confidently.

Maxine walked beside Christine without saying another word, watching her intently. Christine winced as they came out into the hallway's slightly brighter lights.

Maxine held the door open for her and they passed into the large entryway of the manor once again. The bright and natural sunlight from earlier in the day was replaced by the tawny illumination of sconces and chandeliers.

"The dining room is down the hall past the solarium." Maxine pointed to the right, referencing the small sunroom where Christine and Teresa had conversed earlier in the day.

Ahead and to the left, Christine saw the enormous staircase that led to the rooms upstairs. She stopped at the bottom and looked up in awe. The steps were crafted out of white marble and each step had a dark wooden inlay in its center.

"Impressive, isn't it?" Maxine said. "The handrails were hand carved and custom designed for this house."

"Wow!" Christine breathed, mouth gaping at the exquisite sight.

"There is a small elevator in the back of the kitchen that leads to the second and third floors. Would you rather use that?"

Christine reached out and touched the marble banister. It was cold and smooth with an unusual swirl detail embedded. As Christine put one foot on the first step, she suddenly noticed that the air smelled even mustier then it had earlier in the day.

"No, I'd like to try the stairs," Christine whispered softly.

Christine sucked in a deep breath of the thickening air and slowly climbed up one stair after another, the marble feeling strangely familiar under her fingertips.

Once at the top, she turned around and looked down. The stairs yawned back at her. She rested a moment, taking in the span of the second floor.

A very wide hallway wrapped around and flanked the staircase on both sides. Several sconces that had once held candles were now electric and illuminated the hallway. At the top of the stairs, directly in front of her a door was open and with the little bit of light flowing in from hallway, she could tell it was a bathroom. On either side of the bathroom were two large paintings, and on either side of the paintings were large wooden doors.

Maxine stopped at the closed door to the left of the bathroom. From her pocket she withdrew a key and put it in the hole under the glass ball doorknob. With a slight jiggle, the lock clicked easily and Maxine handed the key to Christine. The old fashioned skeleton key felt heavy and jagged in her hand.

"This will be your room," Maxine announced, walking into the dark room. She tugged the pull cord on the tiffany floor lamp near the bed, and then went over to a closet door on the left. She opened it and flicked on the wall switch inside revealing several articles of clothing still sporting price tags, hanging on pink padded hangers.

"I was able to order these this afternoon. We realized that you didn't have time to pack your things, so we took the liberty," Maxine said assumptively.

Maxine crossed the room to open another door on the right. It was the bathroom Christine had seen at the top of the stairs.

"Make yourself comfortable and I'll go down and have Diana fix you a bite to eat," Maxine said as she walked through the bathroom and closed the door to the hallway behind her.

Though the room was dimly lit, Christine was astonished by its luxuriousness. The deep cherry poster bed had a white down comforter with several soft white pillows in front of the ornate embroidered headboard. At the foot of the bed, a long antique lace doily covered a blanket chest. The ceiling-high windows were adorned with yards of white satin curtains embellished with an overlay of more lace. The walls were covered with pale Victorian style wallpaper. Another set of sleep gadgets were in the shadows in the far corner. She took a few steps into the room and was suddenly distracted by a new aroma. The smell of summer flooded the room. She turned around and saw, sitting on the dresser behind the door, a large arrangement of fresh roses and lavender.

Maxine arrived with a hot meal of meatloaf, mashed potatoes, and peas, and Christine found herself famished, again. She quickly finished the meal and decided to run a hot bath before going back to sleep.

She removed her bandages and noticed that the wound appeared to be nearly healed. She poured some scented bubble-bath into the claw foot tub and soaked for a long time in the copious foam. The bath water felt luxurious on her skin. She smiled to herself as she thought the water felt like "liquid pajamas."

After she dried off, she used a large bandage from the medicine chest over the sink to cover the stitches.

She carefully put on the thin, creamy white nightgown and matching robe that she'd taken out of the closet and hung up behind the bathroom door. *Odd,* she thought to herself. *They were the only two articles in the closet that didn't have a store tag on it.*

In the bedroom, she saw that the dinner tray was gone and in its place was a small silver tray with a green mug of hot chocolate topped with a swirl of whipped cream and a plate of three Italian butter cookies.

She drank the smooth, dark brew, ate all three homemade cookies, and immediately dissolved into the soft, cozy bed. She could almost hear the gentle lull of the babbling brook, joined by the symphony of crickets and frogs. The aroma of the lavender and roses made her think of summertime and romance.

Feeling very relaxed and sensual in the soft, flowing nightgown, she was surprised to find herself thinking about Joe. She was anxiously looking forward to seeing him again. She found herself extremely attracted to him. Even though she had only seen him that one time, it wasn't hard for her to recall every detail about him, as if burned into her brain. His hazel eyes and how he looked at her in the hospital. His curly blond, wind-blown hair. His shy, surprised smile. His white teeth, soft lips, strong hands. His muscular shoulders and a spray of dark chest hair under his thin shirt.

The attraction was strong and raw as she started to fall asleep. Christine allowed herself to succumb to the warm, pleasurable thoughts and sensations she began to have when she thought about Joe, without guilt, in the safe, peacefulness of her own dreams.

CHAPTER 14✿

Joe and Shelly returned to the mansion late that night. Shelly had talked non-stop on the plane about all the fun she'd had with Rita - the rides, the food, and the water parks they visited in Orlando. Apparently, the highlight of the trip was a place Rita had found that catered to fairy, elf and leprechaun lovers. There, Shelly had purchased a flowered fairy-like headband and sparkly jewel toned necklace and wore them home on the plane.

At MIRC, the staff warmly greeted them. Maxine and Teresa hugged and fussed over Shelly before she was escorted to her room for the night.

Teresa had eagerly waited for Joe and motioned that they should speak in the library. They walked into the room where a full wall stone fireplace enclosed a roaring fire.

"Can I get you a drink?" she asked, walking towards the small bar in the corner.

"Thanks, I'll get it." Joe walked past her to the bar and reached up to the top shelf and pulled down a dusty, unopened bottle of Divine Caroline Brandy. The crystal bottle was etched with gold and small flecks of diamonds. He wiped off the top with a clean bar towel, opened it gently and poured two glasses.

Teresa was shocked and speechless as she silently accepted the glass he held out to her. The never before opened bottle of brandy was one of the oldest and most expensive in the world. She knew something had happened in Italy.

When she found her voice, Teresa gently asked, "What happened, Joe?"

"*Nothing* happened," he replied as if defeated.

Joe slowly glanced up at the portrait of an elegant woman over the fireplace and spoke as if talking to the picture.

"I tried." Joe raised the brandy glass up to his lips and threw his head back, swallowing the entire contents.

He pulled out of his pocket a well-worn deckled-edged piece of stationary and crumbled it angrily then tossed it towards a trashcan in the corner. He turned to the bar and poured another glass and flopped onto one of the red leather couches.

"I'm sorry. I wish I knew how to help you." Teresa said sincerely. "We've been friends a long time. I know that you went to Italy for personal reasons, and I know that your family's history is over there. If I only knew what is was that you were looking for perhaps I could help…."

"Maybe another time, Teresa, maybe another time. I'm too tired to explain tonight."

Wanting to help Joe, but not knowing how, Teresa regretfully dropped the subject for the evening. However, she was still very excited to tell Joe her news, while he was still sober.

With no regard for the bluntness, Teresa blurted out- "Christine is here! We just moved her to a room upstairs."

The fireplace crackled softly against the steady "tick tock" of the clock on the mantle and Joe looked at Teresa with complete confusion.

She gave him a minute.

"The woman from the hospital?" Joe said, starting to contemplate the importance of the moment. His face opened and sudden interest was back in his body. "Upstairs?"

"I haven't tested her officially, but she's believable, and also has some connection to this town." Teresa sat down on the edge of the chair across from Joe. "Get this! Her grandmother lived in the house on Main Street, the one right in front of the lower gates. I've looked at the family line over and over but I can't find any connection."

Joe noticed the excitement in her voice.

"I'm not sure how she fits into the picture, but there's something about her. She bi-located as sure as I'm standing here…no pun intended." Teresa released a barely audible chuckle at her own joke.

Joe smiled. Teresa was the serious type and she rarely loosened up.

"I bet you couldn't wait to get her on one of your monitors."

"I haven't yet. She's still scared. And she's very…." Teresa paused, trying to find a way to explain. "She likes rules. Rules make her feel safe.

What she's experienced breaks all the rules. This is the first time she's become aware of her talent. She's peppered with low-level psychic abilities, which she's managed to repress due to the negative reactions she experienced as a child, mostly in this town. She thinks she's just lucky."

Teresa had Joe's full attention now, and taking a sip of her brandy, she sat back in the chair.

"Maxine's just informed me that she is starting to have some very lucid dreams, probably prompted by this recent incident. We know these dreams will be a very strong conduit for her repressed memories. However, she claims the bi-location ability has never manifested before. That *is* unusual. As you well know, for the girls, the adolescent and preadolescent hormones typically trigger the dominant trait."

"Yes, I am very aware, but why now? She's obviously not a child. It is so rare to find an adult with new talent."

"I don't know. Something must have triggered it. I'd like to do some blood work on her tomorrow, just to see if anything unusual comes up. And I'd like for Shelly and Christine to meet. I want to be there to observe their interaction."

"Yeah, me too," Joe said.

"Tomorrow then." Teresa said as she left the library.

After Teresa left, Joe got up and poured himself another drink.

With Christine's empty mug and tray in hand, Maxine made her way down to the kitchen. *"Diana will be pleased that our new guest is enjoying her meals,"* she thought.

Maxine noticed the empty liquor glasses in the library and went in to retrieve them. She spotted paper on the floor near the trashcan and picked up the note, intending to discard it into the trash. However, as she picked up the scrap she noticed that the unique, cotton rag stationary seemed vaguely familiar.

The old velvety texture of the personal stationary had been worn down through the years. Maxine noticed the barely visible watermark of the family crest and suddenly remembered where, and when, she had seen this stationary.

It was a very long time ago. She was a little girl. It was the very same stationery that letters to her mother were written on. Against her better judgment, she opened the crumbled note and read it.

To the grandson I will never meet:
Before the end, find the one who got lost and bring her home.
She holds the future of our legacy.
Remember, the strongest traits pass from father to daughter.
God Speed.
Angelina

CHAPTER 15✿

Joe stumbled up the staircase and took a left at the top. He wasn't used to drinking; in fact, he never actually liked the stuff. He was exhausted and disappointed from his trip and his head was starting to spin. He knew he had to hit the bed before the alcohol hit him.

He also knew he was having the symptoms.

Quickly disrobing, Joe climbed into his king sized bed and got under the 1000 sheet count Egyptian cotton bed sheets. He nestled into the downy bed topper.

He could now consider the fact that Christine was *here*. He was all consumed in Italy with the task at hand that he never gave himself a moment to wonder what exactly it was about her that he was gravitating towards. He remembered feeling drawn to her the moment he saw her in the hospital- almost like there was some kind of magnetism or connection between them.

Certainly, she was beautiful. Sweet. Innocent. He could not deny that he felt an attraction to her immediately. It had been a long time since he had been with a woman. His heart began to race and he felt the warm sensations settle in from the alcohol. Joe let go of his inhibitions and followed his fantasies into the impending fuzzy dream world.

CHAPTER 16✿

      Early in the morning, Christine woke up to the sound of hushed, excited voices and the patter of running on threadbare carpeting coming from the hallway outside of her bedroom. She shrank under the covers, shrouded immediately by a vintage memory.

      She recoiled, feeling the emotional sting as she remembered a time when she went to play at the park down the street from her grandmother's house. It was the very first time she was picked on and teased. They treated her like she was different. Since then, she had learned not to tell of the things that she knew. But that sad memory flooded back to her this morning.

      She hesitantly dressed and went downstairs. As she reached the bottom of the steps, no longer was there musty smells. The scent of fresh coffee and bacon now inundated the air and erased the foggy, painful memory. She heard the chatter coming from down the hall. She was hungry and headed toward the stimulating aromas coming from the dining room.

As she turned the corner and entered the bright, sunlit morning room, the giggling and playing ceased, and silence, like a wet blanket, hung in the air.

Two boys and one girl, each about ten or eleven years old, were sitting on one side of a long, polished cherry wood table. They were staring at her. Across the room, Teresa was standing near a long buffet table pouring a cup of coffee from a silver coffeepot.

Suddenly, Joe entered through a doorway behind Teresa. Christine, caught completely off guard, quickly sucked in air and felt her heart race in her chest.

Joe paused when he saw Christine. Their eyes locked, and each held the glance longer than appropriate. A sudden tingle surged down Christine's spine. His eyes were staring at her so intently, as if he could read her thoughts. She finally averted her eyes and felt her face get hot with embarrassment as she instantly recalled the familiar and extremely sensual dream she'd had of him last night.

"Hey…. it's you!" a voice excitedly called out.

It was then that Christine saw the blond haired girl who had been sitting with her back to her. She immediately recognized the girl from the plane.

The two stared at each other for a second. Then Shelly suddenly jumped from her seat, ran over, and hugged Christine tightly around the waist.

Christine stiffened at first because her first instinct was to protect her wound but she instantly realized that the hug caused no pain at all, and she warmly returned the hug. She looked up at Joe and

Teresa, observing the encounter. The intensity of Joe's stare made Christine extremely uncomfortable.

"I'm Shelly," the girl said finally, pulling back from Christine. "And these are my friends, Paul, Patrick, and Margie."

Finding their voices the children clamored in unison, "Hi!"

So these are the children I heard. They look healthy enough. Why are they here? Why do they need to be in a convalescent manor? Christine wondered.

"Good morning, Chris." Joe motioned with his hands to the buffet but his eyes never left Christine's. "Welcome. Please come and have some breakfast," he said.

Teresa poured a second cup of coffee and handed it to her.

The food on the buffet was bountiful. Scrambled eggs, bacon, toast, muffins, fruit, even a small quiche. All displayed on beautiful white china on linen table runners.

Christine could feel the steely eyes in the room on her back. She could tell they all knew about her. They were all watching her, studying her, like some kind of strange insect.

Suddenly she wasn't feeling all that hungry anymore.

Shelly patted loudly on the seat next to hers, leaving no doubt that she wanted Christine to sit down next to her and across from the wide eyed stares of the other children. Joe and Teresa did not sit, but watched intensely from the corner.

Christine took her coffee and sat down next to Shelly.

"Oh!" Christine's foot hit something under the table and it slid across the floor towards the boys. "Sorry. What was that?" she asked, looking under the eyelet embellished tablecloth.

"It's a warming pad for your feet," Shelly said over the giggles of the other three children. "There's one for each of us. You can slip off your shoes and put your feet on it so you stay warm, 'cause of the cold tile floors."

The two boys were squirming in their chairs, taking the opportunity to play a quick game. They peered under the table and stretched their legs, each trying to reach the pad first. Quickly it sailed back across to Christine, who, without looking, expertly caught the heated pillow with both feet.

The tall, dark haired boy, clearly assuming he'd been the winner of the new game, started the questioning first.

"Did you really project yourself?" Paul said through his mouth full of eggs and toast.

"Don't talk with your mouth full! That's gross!" Margie piped in, obviously disgusted with crumbs dropping back onto Paul's plate from his mouth.

"Yeah, what was it like? Was it like a wind tunnel?" Patrick, the smaller of the two boys asked, his eyes wide.

"Sorry," Joe said to Christine. "News travels fast around here," he added and turned a raised eyebrow to his daughter.

"I just knew she'd be here when we got back, I just knew it!" Shelly happily exclaimed to her father.

"Clearly she's thrilled to see Christine here," Joe whispered to Teresa.

Wiping his mouth with the back of his hand, Paul announced, "No one's ever really done that, I mean, for real."

Patrick, who was sitting directly across from Christine, was staring down at his half empty plate, with dark eyes growing large as his pupils nearly filled up his eyeballs.

"Look what I can do!" Patrick quickly and proudly announced as his fork suddenly levitated about twelve inches above his plate.

Christine let out a cry of surprise as she slid her chair backwards over the slippery marble floor.

"Show-off! You're in big trouble now!" yelled Shelly.

"You're not supposed to do that here!" shrieked Margie. "We're only allowed to do stuff in the classroom- never outside the classroom! Stop it!"

The commotion ended with gasps as the fork crashed down, chipping the china plate.

"All right, that's enough!" Teresa stepped forward, her voice firm and assertive. "Children, clear your places and go right to class. Patrick, you had better bring that dish to Chef Diana straight away and then see me in the library." Glaring at him, she continued, "We have rules for a reason!"

"Yeah, if there *is* a teacher in class today!" whispered Paul to Margie.

Overhearing Paul, Joe asked, "The problem with Mrs. Brenner hasn't been resolved yet?" mild irritation in his voice.

"We're still working on that." Teresa answered, not taking her eyes off of Patrick.

On her way out, Shelly bent over and whispered to Christine, "I can do better than that. I'll come see you after my classes." Then she spun out of the room.

Patrick put the broken chip on the plate then gathered up the rest of his silverware carefully and started towards the door where Teresa and Joe were standing.

"I'm really sorry," he said sincerely to them as he passed.

"Please apologize to our guest. You've startled her," Teresa said firmly.

"I'm sorry Miss Smith. I'm sorry if I scared you," Patrick apologized.

Christine, face ashen, just nodded as the boy left the room.

"Are you sure you don't want anything to eat?" Joe motioned again to the buffet, acting as if nothing out of the ordinary had happened.

Christine ignored his question, too full of her own.

"What just happened? How did he do that?" she cried. "*What's wrong with the children? How….*"

"We have something to tell you," Teresa interrupted.

Teresa brought Christine a plate with a blueberry muffin and some fresh fruit, then sat down in the chair Shelly had vacated.

"Joe," she said. "She needs to know."

CHAPTER 17✾

"… so the initials of MIRC don't really stand for Medical Intensive Recovery Center. The initials represent Memory, Intuition, Research and Communication," Teresa finally revealed to Christine.

Christine sat and listened quietly, trying to understand what she had just been told.

"So you're saying that these children are perfectly normal and healthy, but you are studying them, doing *research* on them?!" Christine was pallid as she tried to accept this incredible information.

"The children are called 'Sensitives'. They possess, in some amount, psychometric, telepathic, clairvoyant or other psychic traits and skills. We simply help them tune into and develop these skills. Our mission at MIRC is for them to eventually learn to control their abilities," Teresa responded. "We teach them to recognize proper situations in which to use their skills."

"We've found that when you decrease the barriers surrounding the conscience mind, you can increase the conduits for ESP, premonition and intuition." Joe added. "And our other goal is, of course, to protect them from outside harm and abuse."

Christine turned angrily to Joe. She felt like he'd somehow lied and betrayed her,

"What about you, Joe? What's your part in all of this?"

From the doorway behind Joe, Maxine quietly padded her way into the room, excused herself past him and started to collect the dishes on the buffet.

"My grandmother was a Precog, which means that she knew about things that hadn't happened yet. Both of her parents also had the gifts. They were both born in Italy and eventually came over to America and settled here on this hill.

"They were never really accepted in this town. My grandmother..." Joe paused, trying to explain. "She tried to use her gift to help others but too many people feared and resented her for it.

"She opened the house up to those who wanted and needed the help under the guise of the Medical Intensive Recovery Center. Eventually, my parents started doing the real work of the center and with the help of people like Teresa, located those with gifts like yours who needed protection, help and guidance."

"The children are here because they, like you, have special traits." Teresa added, pausing a moment to allow the information to sink in. "We protect them and teach them how to cope with and use their talents."

"For whatever reason, you and my daughter connected." Joe said. "My daughter may have been in danger on that plane and somehow you knew it and were there to protect her. I am forever grateful to you for that. It also seems that she's immediately bonded to you like no one else I've ever seen her with."

Teresa got up from the table.

"We would like to do some tests this morning-with your permission, of course."

Maxine had been waiting for instructions on preparing the testing from Teresa. Suddenly she stiffened and had a blank far away stare on her face.

"Maxine, are you alright? You look pale." Teresa moved towards her.

Maxine, cocked her head to one side, turned her stare towards Christine. The plate of toast she held tipped and the bread fell onto the floor.

"I'm so... sorry," Maxine stuttered, bending down to pick up the toast. "Yes, I'm fine. Would you like for me to set up the tests, Teresa?"

Shaking her head with slight annoyance, Teresa turned to Christine once again and waited for her answer.

"What kinds of tests?"

"Just some simple blood tests, maybe an EKG. We don't do highly invasive procedures here. And I'd like to talk with you some more to see if we can get you to remember anything else."

"O.k., if that's all." Christine agreed.

"Maxine..?" Teresa called.

Maxine was again staring curiously at Christine.

"Maxine. Can you get the materials ready for the blood work?" Teresa asked in a slightly firmer tone.

"Yes, sorry. I'll get right to it." Maxine shook her head as if to try to focus on her duties. She finished cleaning up and followed the other three out of the room.

❀ ❀ ❀ ❀ ❀ ❀

After the blood was drawn, Teresa continued to question Christine.

"Maxine mentioned that you have been having some dreams lately."

"Actually, yes. I haven't had these kinds of vivid dreams since I was a little girl. But it seems like since coming here, they've started again."

"Can you remember any?" "Teresa asked coaxingly.

As hard as she tried, she couldn't shake off the dream she had last night about Joe and while it was front and foremost on her mind, she could *never* reveal the very private nature of *that* dream.

"Yes, I remember the one Maxine mentioned to you. Two children, a boy and a girl, were going to ambush another little boy entering this property from the gates at the bottom of the hill. They were hiding in the bushes, and when another little boy entered the property, they pelted him with rocks."

"Go on," Teresa encouraged her.

"I saw myself in the dream. I was a child too, and ran up to the little boy to protect him. He was bleeding from his forehead where they had already hit him with a rock. I could hear the boy and girl who threw the rocks giggling in the bushes and I was very sad that they were so mean."

"Anything else?"

"Well, when I tried to protect the boy he looked at me and ran away like he was afraid of me, even though I was trying to help him."

"How did the dream end?"

"My side started to ache and in the dream I looked down and I was bleeding from the same place that I'd been shot. Here." She pointed to her side. "And the boy in the bushes didn't want me to tell our mother."

"*Our mother?*"

"Yeah, he called me by another name, and asked if I was going to tell mom?"

"What name did he call you?" Teresa pressed.

"I don't remember, Maxine came and I woke up."

There was a long silence before Teresa replied.

"Dreams may hold the answers to questions we haven't even asked yet," Teresa finally said. "Let me know right away if you have any more unusual dreams. Try to remember the little details- they are often the key."

"Why are you so interested in my dreams?"

"Well, during altered states of consciousness like meditation or sleep we believe the brain accesses other areas not yet understood."

"And that's what the monitors in the rooms are used for- dreaming and sleeping?"

"Yes."

Without wanting to get too technical, Teresa switched gears and asked, "Christine, are you sure you have never experienced any bi-location before, not even as a child?"

"No, but I remember something else, now that we're talking about dreams. A few times when I was a child and had those extremely vivid dreams, sometimes I'd wake up dirty. There'd be like, dirt on my feet and leaves or sticks in my hair and bed. My mother was convinced that I was sneaking out during the night. I told her I wasn't but she didn't believe me. She started locking my door at night to punish me and to be sure."

"How old were you?"

"About twelve or so. I don't really remember much, just that it happened a few times after that but I cleaned up before my mother saw. My dad was very sick and I didn't want her to worry about me. Shortly after that my father died and we moved away."

"Nothing unusual after the move?"

"No. Nothing that I can remember. I had an opportunity to start fresh and I didn't let myself stand out so the teasing stopped."

"Alright, then. Let's see what the blood work shows, if anything. Why don't you rest and we'll talk later."

"Okay," Christine said watching Teresa walk out of the solarium.

The sun was shining brightly through the glass-enclosed room making it warm. Christine walked over to the window and looked out at the cold landscape watching drops of melting snow drip down still-frozen icicles above the arched window. From here she could see the road leading down the hill. No longer covered by the hard packed snow, patches of wispy white powder blew across parts of the black, glistening road.

She opened the window a crack to let in some moist, cold air. Bushes under the window sagged with the weight of the snow like half opened umbrellas.

Crows were flying overhead, landing in the trees. They sounded like cats fighting. Over their cries, Christine could hear the children playing outside.

This would be a great place to sleigh ride, she thought, fondly remembering this fun winter event. She remembered how her legs, nose, and cheeks got so cold that they felt like they were burning. She closed her eyes, smelling the snow through the open window.

A door opened, and Christine heard someone quickly coming down the hallway.

"Hi!" Shelly said as she skipped into the room toward Christine, hugging her again.

Immediately, Christine warmly returned the hug.

"There has got to be some connection, Joe," Teresa said, pulling out paperwork from a red file folder and tossing the smaller manila folders onto the library table. "Christine just admitted that she had unexplained events when she was a child, and has reported a history of lucid dreams. We need to get her on those monitors as soon as possible. In any event, there's got to be something here. Look, this is the history of the town and its families."

Joe recalled the *very* lucid dream he'd had about Christine last night too, and attributed it to the unaccustomed liquor. He rushed to the conference table and looked over Teresa's shoulder at the papers.

"This is what I have on Christine's family tree."

Teresa pulled out a chart from a folder.

"Christine's parents were Anthony Smith and Maggie Russell. Anthony Smith's parents were William Smith and Tina Regina. Now, Tina Regina-Smith was Christine's grandmother, the one who lived in the small house at the bottom of this hill. From what I can see, she has no special history within the town and there's no information that anything unique was ever disclosed about her. She married William Smith, who moved down from Connecticut to live here in this town. What am I missing? Do you see any connection?"

Before Joe could answer, Maxine entered the room.

"Excuse me," Maxine interrupted. She handed some papers to Teresa. "I have some results from the blood work."

❀ ❀ ❀ ❀ ❀ ❀

"I told you I'd come visit. Boy, Patrick sure is a show-off, isn't he?" Shelly was sitting as close to Christine as she could on the couch.

"Well, I don't..." Christine wasn't sure what to say to this young girl. "What is it that you can do, exactly?"

"I'm a telekinetic. I can move things with my mind. Patrick is one too, but I'm better."

"Are you all telekinetic?"

"No, Margie is a psychometric."

"What's that?"

"She can touch something and tell you about the person that it belonged to. And Paul is a retrocog. Sometimes they call him the one with the second sight. That means he can see things that took place in the past *and* he has many people inside of him. He can go into a trance and become another person for a few minutes." Excited to be able to tell someone about her friends, Shelly continued. "Just me and Patrick can move things. I got it from my father but Patrick doesn't have a family gene like I do."

"What do you mean you got it from your father? *Joe* can move things too?"

"No, just the girls in my family can do things. Our special traits are passed down and the traits are the strongest when they get passed from father to daughter. My dad doesn't have any special signs of the trait but he passed it on to me. My grandfather carried the gene and passed it to my father who passed it to me. The boys are called "vessels" or "carries". Only the girls can use their secret. It's been in my dad's family for lots of generations.

"My great, great grandparents came over from Italy years ago and built this house. Maybe you've heard of them. Antonio and Philomena Bernardo?" Shelly asked proudly as if to imply perhaps her grandparents were famous enough for Christine to have heard of. "They *both* had the genes. And they lived here in this house." Pausing only long enough to catch her breath, she quickly added, "Maybe your father passed the secret on to you?"

"No," Christine answered, shaking her head. "I don't have anything like that in my family."

"Maybe you could ask him?"

"No, I can't. My father passed away when I was about your age."

"Oh," and without hesitation, in true childlike behavior asked, "how did he die?'

"Suddenly," Christina answered, "He never showed any signs of being ill. It was some rare disease that didn't show any symptoms. He was sick but I didn't know he was dying. His disease wasn't seen on the outside of his body. No one knew he was sick," she explained.

Their conversation was interrupted by a stampede of feet as the other three children raced into the room.

"Hey, Shelly? Can we visit too?" Patrick asked out of breath.

"Sure, but no tricks! You've already scared her today," Shelly replied.

All three settled on the couch looking at Christine with their bright rosy cheeks and red noses glowing on their little white faces.

"Promise," Patrick said. "Can you beam yourself somewhere again?"

"Beam myself?" Christine giggled. "I never even knew that I could do this before, and I don't think I can do it again."

"I bet you can," Margie said. "They can help you here. That's why we're all here, so that we can get good at what we do."

"Teresa helps us learn how to control our abilities," Patrick chimed in.

"You didn't do such a good job of controlling *your* ability this morning," Margie brought to his attention sarcastically.

"Yeah, but a least you can *see* what I can do," Patrick replied, taunting Margie.

Margie's face tightened and she glared at Patrick, but before she could think of something to say back, Christine interrupted.

"Margie, what is it that you can do? Shelly told me you touch things and something happens?"

Pleased to talk about it, Margie replied, "Patrick's right. You can't *see* what I can do but I'm getting really good at it. When I go back home I'll be able to control it, better that Patrick." Margie stuck her tongue out at Patrick and continued.

"When I touch things I pick up on feelings and I see little pictures about the person who owned the item. My parents own a little antique store in South Carolina and at first I didn't know what was wrong with me because when I would go in and play, especially with the jewelry, all of the pictures in my head came at me all at once," Margie waived her arms around in front of her.

"Then Teresa came out to see us and brought me here to help me. She helps me to focus so I'm not having it all happen around me all at once," Margie finished.

"We are protected here, no one can hurt us or know about us so that we can practice and get better." Paul said.

"What happens then?" Christine asked.

"We go back to our families and we are allowed to practice by ourselves…." Paul answered, but Patrick quickly interrupted.

"I heard we can go to school and be *distractors!*"

Shelly jumped to the edge of the sofa. "They don't *want* you to be a distractor!" she said to Patrick. "They don't want us to stand out and if you are a distractor you can get caught!"

"I wouldn't get caught!" Patrick retorted back.

Christine was confused, "What's a distractor?"

"One of us does something in class to create a distraction so that another kid can do something else, like play a joke on the teacher, without the teacher finding out," Paul answered.

"But if you're good, you don't get caught, and I'm good so I won't!' Patrick insisted.

"Are you going to stay with us?" Shelly asked, changing the subject quickly. "You'll be able to do it again, Teresa can teach you."

"No, I don't think so. I live in Sara--"

The words came out of her mouth before she realized what she had said. She knew in her heart that she wasn't ever going back to Florida.

❀ ❀ ❀ ❀ ❀ ❀

"The blood work shows she's anemic," Teresa mumbled, quickly reading out loud through the lab sheet. "And... the anti-nuclear antibody... her ANA is elevated, just like yours and Shelly's!" Teresa said with surprise.

"A coincidence, I'm sure." Joe said, convincingly.

"An extremely *rare* coincidence!"

Maxine stood fast where she was in the doorway.

Joe looked up. "Maxine, is there something?" he asked curiously.

Maxine took a long, deep breath before she started to speak yet still tripped over her words.

"Joe, I stumbled upon, found this, ah, note." She held out the aged note she found near the trash, face reddening.

Joe glanced down at the paper that Maxine held out.

"It's nothing, Maxine. Just garbage. Throw it away. I don't need it," Joe said.

Maxine didn't move. "I'm sorry Joe, but I read the note."

"It's okay, Maxine." Joe said, accepting her apology. But in a slightly more irritated tone continued, "I told you it isn't important anymore, just throw it away."

Stretching her arm out, she tried to hand him the aged paper, the wrinkles neatly pressed out.

"I think there's something you should know. I think this might have something to do with Christine," Maxine finally said.

Teresa snatched the note from Maxine's outstretched hand and looked at Joe, waiting for an explanation.

"Look," he said to Teresa, "That note was left for me by my grandmother. She said to find 'the lost one'. *That's* why I went to Italy, to see if any other family members are still alive. There are none left. There are no other blood relatives alive."

Maxine interrupted. "My mother was your mother's confidante, Joe. She received letters on that stationary from your grandmother. I recognized that stationary."

"What in the world does this have to do with Christine?" Teresa angrily asked Maxine.

"My mother was your grandmother's friend and she trusted her," Maxine explained to Joe. "They shared secrets and told each other everything. You know my family has always been entrusted with confidential information."

"Go on."

"One day I read one of the letters from your grandmother."

"Okay, Maxine, what did it say?" Joe's frustration and impatience was showing.

"Well," Maxine paused and looked out the window off in the distance as if trying to see the letter in the snow. "It was about Carmine Bernardo."

"Your great uncle, your grandmother's brother, right Joe?" Teresa asked.

Joe nodded.

"The letter from your grandmother said that she thought Carmine had an affair with Tina Regina, Christine's grandmother, while she was married to Smith, and that Tina had Carmine's baby but could never reveal this."

Teresa's mind was racing. She ran over to the papers on the round conference table and scattered through them until she pulled one out, pushing all of the others away.

"Teresa?" Joe asked.

In all of the years Joe had known Teresa, she had never raised her voice and never lost her composure until now.

"NO! Look here! Here are the family trees. There are no records of Carmine ever fathering a child!" Teresa shrieked. "Remember? He never even married and died suddenly. This is the first time anyone has heard of this." She turned to Maxine.

"Maxine, are you sure... absolutely sure that's what you read?"

"Yes. I think Christine has family blood in her veins."

The three of them looked back and forth at each other and the mapped out family tree, trying to put the pieces all together.

"If this is true, then it all makes sense." Teresa finally said. Looking over at Joe, she gasped, "Joe, she's your cousin!"

"*She's* the lost one!" Joe whispered softly.

CHAPTER 18❀

Once he had confirmation from the rest of the blood work, Joe knew what he had to do. He just wasn't sure how to do it or if Christine would accept. He could tell that she was not a bad or greedy person, or she would have used her "luckiness" to get rich. No, he'd decided, she was not inclined to gain wealth or power. What was it then that she would want?

That night he watched in awe as the children and Christine giggled and laughed together over dinner. He had never seen these children or even his own daughter getting along with anyone so easily before.

After dinner, Joe waited for Christine in the library. He stood up from where he was seated on the leather sofa in front of the fire when Maxine ushered Christine in.

"Hi, Chris. Please, have a seat," he said motioning to the sofa. "Maxine, please close the door behind you."

The door made a hollow sound as Maxine did as he'd asked.

Instead, Christine sat in a burgundy leather chair directly across from the sofa and adjacent to the fireplace. She gazed into the burning embers, mesmerized by the haunting glow from within the logs. A pop, then a blast of orange cinders flew out of the logs and swirled up into the chimney.

Joe walked toward the liquor decanters on the table in the corner.

"Teresa told me you're off the pain meds. Would you like a drink?" The ice in his own glass clinked together as he set it down on the counter

"No, thank you. I don't drink," she said shyly.

"I'm glad you're feeling better, though a bit surprised that you suddenly have no more pain."

"I'm surprised by it, too. One day it was terrible and the next day it was completely gone."

Joe walked around and sat down on the arm of the sofa, directly across from her. She had not been alone with him since the day they met in the hospital. She didn't know why, but before, she had feared looking directly into his eyes. Now, Christine looked deeply into his eyes.

She was suddenly frightened by what she saw.

His eyes compelled her, and she found him returning her stare a little too long. Suddenly feeling very uncomfortable, she averted her eyes.

"Who's that?" Christine motioned to the portrait above the mantel, anxious to divert his eyes from her.

"Funny you should ask. That is my grandmother, Angelina Pasquali."

"Angelina?" Christine repeated, and tilted her head as if trying to remember where she'd heard that name before.

"Chris, we found out something about you today that you need to know." Still not knowing how to say it, he stammered, "I knew there was something about you when we first met in the hospital. I thought that maybe I'd seen you before, before the news, that is. I also thought that maybe the feeling as if I knew you was because I'd seen you on the plane the day Shelly did."

"I had the same feelings about you." Christine said, surprised. She quickly wondered if they were both also talking romantic feelings.

"Now I think I may know why," he said, pointing to the painting. "We are related. Angelina was my grandmother and your great aunt. We have the same great grandmother."

Joe waited and watched Christine take in the startling information.

"What?" Christine said with an uncomfortable giggle as she found the information incredulous. "That's ridiculous!"

"Maxine and Teresa did some additional tests on your blood. They believe that we are something like second generation cousins."

"That's impossible! How can that be?"

Joe walked over to the small conference table and pulled out a neatly folded piece of paper. "Chris, come over and have a look," he said.

Christine looked at the family tree document, which looked worn but official.

"We believe that it is possible that your grandmother Tina had an affair with my great uncle.

Your father's father was my great uncle, Carmine Bernardo. You received your gift through your father who carried the gene from Carmine."

"Carmine?" Christine repeated the name, and suddenly she recalled the dream she relayed to Teresa.

"Your grandmother could never risk exposing the secret to anyone," Joe continued. My family was not kindly accepted in this town, as I've mentioned to you before, for the reasons stated. To protect herself and your father, she never revealed the secret. My great grandmother, Angelina, because she was a precog, knew *something* but not enough to be positive. She did know that there would be another in our family possessing a strong trait. She left a sealed note only to be opened by her great grand-son, that's me. Since Teresa had no evidence of any more of my family here in the states, I went to Italy in search of the family line and turned up short.

"I know this is a shock right now. But isn't it better to know who you really are? It explains why you have the gifts and where they came from." Christine was very still and quiet, hardly breathing, as she tried to absorb what he was saying.

"We want you to stay on with us, Chris. Teresa found out you have a teaching degree. We've had, for obvious reasons, some problems with maintaining a teacher for the children. They aren't told the real reasons why the children are here and sometime get 'spooked' when the children act up-like this morning.

"The children like you, and now that you understand that they have abilities such as your own, they would benefit greatly from your staying on with us."

Christine was extremely confused. She finally found some words.

"You're offering me a job?"

"A job, yes. And we can help you hone your own skills. We really need you here... *I* really need you to stay," Joe pleaded.

"There's more, isn't there?" Christine noted his desperation. "What is it?"

"Chris, I don't have very much time. Shelly needs someone around who will understand her. Someone like her. Someone who is family. *You* are her only family. The men in our family genetically carry the traits, which not only pass to the females so that they can express a special trait, but in the males the gene also harbors a disease of which there is no cure. I think that your father died of the same disease I have. My doctor recently informed me that I don't have much more time."

"Oh, God, I'm so sorry, Joe!" Christine immediately felt a lump in her throat. "I don't know what to say...."

"I need to ask you if you would be Shelly's guardian."

"Guardian?" Christine jumped up and paced around the room.

"I don't know, I don't know! This is all so sudden!"

"You don't have to give me an answer right now. I know this is a lot to accept. It's just that all this makes sense to me now."

Christine was filled with compassion. She knew in her heart that Joe was a good man, and this was a good man's dying wish. He wanted his daughter protected. Christine looked into his eyes and felt the answer swell up into her throat.

FIVE MONTHS LATER

It was hot when Christine and Shelly slowly advanced up the hill to the cemetery. A light breeze blew old brown leaves up in front of them like antiqued pieces of newspaper turning over and over.

"I'm really, really glad you stayed. I'm glad you're here to look after me."

"I am too, Shelly," Christine said, embracing the feeling of acceptance.

They stood looking down at the grave. Shelly held a crystal vase of water. She handed Christine a pair of scissors from the back pocket of her shorts.

Closing her eyes as the storm in her ears escalated with the rise of her blood pressure, Christine reached out with both hands in front of her and using the scissors, cut into the air with her right hand. Stem after stem of bright red hibiscus flowers appeared in her left. She hadn't yet learned how to control the pain in her head with the purposeful actions, but the hour of discomfort that was to follow was a relatively small price to pay. She handed the bunch to Shelly, who promptly plopped them into the water-filled vase.

"My dad always said I was special. It's okay, you know, to be different," Shelly said to her.

"Why be normal when you can be special, right?" Christine responded.

Christine took a deep breath and again closed her eyes and turned slightly to her left. Once more, she reached out with the scissors into nothing but air, but this time the scissors fell. Her eyes still closed, she picked them up and again out of the air, four beautiful white orchids appear in her left hand.

"Those are beautiful!" Shelly exclaimed. "What are they?" she asked with wide eyes.

"These are ghost orchids. This particular variety is very expensive. Did you know that some orchids only bloom under the most perfect conditions?" She held them out so Shelly could smell them. "They need lots of TLC to grow this beautiful. These are perfect because they were cared for on a protected and specially designed property." Christine said proudly, wiping the Florida sand off of the scissors.

"Have you picked a name yet?"

"Yes," Christine replied confidently. "Your sister's name will be Angelina," she said, resting her hand against her gently swollen belly.

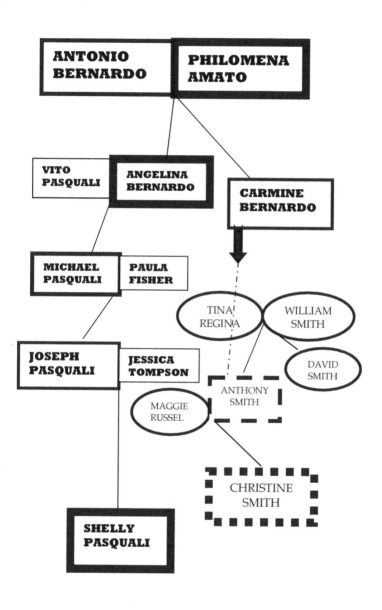

Made in the USA
Middletown, DE
09 June 2019